PENGUIN ARCHIVE
Revenge

Vladimir Nabokov
1899–1977
A PENGUIN SINCE 1960

Vladimir Nabokov
Revenge

PENGUIN ARCHIVE

PENGUIN BOOKS

UK | USA | Canada | Ireland | Australia
India | New Zealand | South Africa

Penguin Books is part of the Penguin Random House group of companies whose addresses can be found at global.penguinrandomhouse.com.

Penguin Random House UK,
One Embassy Gardens, 8 Viaduct Gardens, London SW11 7BW

penguin.co.uk

Selected from *Collected Stories*, first published by G. P. Putnam's Sons, New York 1965
Reissued in Penguin Classics 2010
This selection published in Penguin Classics 2025
003

Copyright © Article 3c under the will of Vladimir Nabokov, 1965, 1966

Most of the stories in this volume were originally written in Russian, with English translations prepared by Vladimir and Dmitri Nabokov. See *Collected Stories* for more details.

No part of this book may be used or reproduced in any manner for the purpose of training artificial intelligence technologies or systems. In accordance with Article 4(3) of the DSM Directive 2019/790, Penguin Random House expressly reserves this work from the text and data mining exception.

Set in 11.2/13.75pt Dante MT Std
Typeset by Jouve (UK), Milton Keynes
Printed and bound in Great Britain by Clays Ltd, Elcograf S.p.A.

The authorized representative in the EEA is Penguin Random House Ireland, Morrison Chambers, 32 Nassau Street, Dublin D02 YH68

A CIP catalogue record for this book is available from the British Library

ISBN: 978–0–241–74700–1

Penguin Random House is committed to a sustainable future for our business, our readers and our planet. This book is made from Forest Stewardship Council® certified paper.

Contents

Details of a Sunset	1
The Thunderstorm	13
A Nursery Tale	19
Easter Rain	39
The Dragon	51
Revenge	61
A Forgotten Poet	71
The Seaport	89
Razor	99
First Love	105
The Wood-Sprite	117
Music	123
Perfection	133

Details of a Sunset

The last streetcar was disappearing in the mirrorlike murk of the street and, along the wire above it, a spark of Bengal light, crackling and quivering, sped into the distance like a blue star.

'Well, might as well just plod along, even though you are pretty drunk, Mark, pretty drunk . . .'

The spark went out. The roofs glistened in the moonlight, silvery angles broken by oblique black cracks.

Through this mirrory darkness he staggered home: Mark Standfuss, a salesclerk, a demigod, fair-haired Mark, a lucky fellow with a high starched collar. At the back of his neck, above the white line of that collar, his hair ended in a funny, boyish little tag that had escaped the barber's scissors. That little tag was what made Klara fall in love with him, and she swore that it was true love, that she had quite forgotten the handsome ruined foreigner who last year had rented a room from her mother, Frau Heise.

'And yet, Mark, you're drunk . . .'

That evening there had been beer and songs with friends in honor of Mark and russet-haired, pale Klara, and in a week they would be married; then there would be a lifetime of bliss and peace, and of nights with her, the red blaze of her hair spreading all over the pillow, and, in the morning, again her quiet laughter, the green dress, the coolness of her bare arms.

In the middle of a square stood a black wigwam: the tram tracks were being repaired. He remembered how today he had got under her short sleeve, and kissed the touching scar from her smallpox vaccination. And now he was walking home, unsteady on his feet from too much happiness and too much drink, swinging his slender cane, and among the dark houses on the opposite side of the empty street a night echo clop-clopped in time with his footfalls; but grew silent when he turned at the corner where the same man as always, in apron and peaked cap, stood by his grill, selling frankfurters, crying out in a tender and sad birdlike whistle: '*Würstchen, würstchen . . .*'

Mark felt a sort of delicious pity for the frankfurters, the moon, the blue spark that had receded along the wire, and, as he tensed his body against a friendly fence, he was overcome with laughter, and, bending, exhaled into a little round hole in the boards the words 'Klara, Klara, oh my darling!'

On the other side of the fence, in a gap between the buildings, was a rectangular vacant lot. Several moving vans stood there like enormous coffins. They were bloated from their loads. Heaven knows what was piled inside them. Oakwood trunks, probably, and chandeliers like iron spiders, and the heavy skeleton of a double bed. The moon cast a hard glare on the vans. To the left of the lot, huge black hearts were flattened against a bare

Details of a Sunset

rear wall – the shadows, many times magnified, of the leaves of a linden tree that stood next to a streetlamp on the edge of the sidewalk.

Mark was still chuckling as he climbed the dark stairs to his floor. He reached the final step, but mistakenly raised his foot again, and it came down awkwardly with a bang. While he was groping in the dark in search of the keyhole, his bamboo cane slipped out from under his arm and, with a subdued little clatter, slid down the staircase. Mark held his breath. He thought the cane would turn with the stairs and knock its way down to the bottom. But the high-pitched wooden click abruptly ceased. Must have stopped. He grinned with relief and, holding on to the banister (the beer singing in his hollow head), started to descend again. He nearly fell, and sat down heavily on a step, as he groped around with his hands.

Upstairs the door onto the landing opened. Frau Standfuss, with a kerosene lamp in her hand, half-dressed, eyes blinking, the haze of her hair showing from beneath her nightcap, came out and called, 'Is that you, Mark?'

A yellow wedge of light encompassed the banisters, the stairs, and his cane, and Mark, panting and pleased, climbed up again to the landing, and his black, hunchbacked shadow followed him up along the wall.

Then, in the dimly lit room, divided by a red screen, the following conversation took place:

'You've had too much to drink, Mark.'

'No, no, Mother . . . I'm so happy . . .'

'You've got yourself all dirty, Mark. Your hand is black . . .'

'. . . so very happy . . . Ah, that feels good . . . water's nice and cold. Pour some on the top of my head . . . more . . . Everybody congratulated me, and with good reason . . . Pour some more on.'

'But they say she was in love with somebody else such a short time ago – a foreign adventurer of some kind. Left without paying five marks he owed Frau Heise . . .'

'Oh, stop – you don't understand anything . . . We did such a lot of singing today . . . Look, I've lost a button . . . I think they'll double my salary when I get married . . .'

'Come on, go to bed . . . You're all dirty, and your new pants too.'

That night Mark had an unpleasant dream. He saw his late father. His father came up to him, with an odd smile on his pale, sweaty face, seized Mark under the arms, and began to tickle him silently, violently, and relentlessly.

He only remembered that dream after he had arrived at the store where he worked, and he remembered it because a friend of his, jolly Adolf, poked him in the ribs. For one instant something flew open in his soul, momentarily froze still in surprise, and slammed shut. Then again everything became easy and limpid, and the neckties he offered his customers smiled brightly, in sympathy with his happiness. He knew he would see Klara that evening – he would only run home for dinner, then go straight to her house . . . The other day, when he was telling her how cozily and tenderly they would live, she had suddenly burst into tears. Of course Mark had understood that these were tears of joy (as she herself

Details of a Sunset

explained); she began whirling about the room, her skirt like a green sail, and then she started rapidly smoothing her glossy hair, the color of apricot jam, in front of the mirror. And her face was pale and bewildered, also from happiness, of course. It was all so natural, after all . . .

'A striped one? Why certainly.'

He knotted the tie on his hand, and turned it this way and that, enticing the customer. Nimbly he opened the flat cardboard boxes . . .

Meanwhile his mother had a visitor: Frau Heise. She had come without warning, and her face was tear-stained. Gingerly, almost as if she were afraid of breaking into pieces, she lowered herself onto a stool in the tiny, spotless kitchen where Frau Standfuss was washing the dishes. A two-dimensional wooden pig hung on the wall, and a half-open matchbox with one burnt match lay on the stove.

'I have come to you with bad news, Frau Standfuss.'

The other woman froze, clutching a plate to her chest.

'It's about Klara. Yes. She has lost her senses. That lodger of mine came back today – you know, the one I told you about. And Klara has gone mad. Yes, it all happened this morning . . . She never wants to see your son again . . . You gave her the material for a new dress; it will be returned to you. And here is a letter for Mark. Klara's gone mad. I don't know what to think . . .'

Meanwhile Mark had finished work and was already on his way home. Crew-cut Adolf walked him all the way to his house. They both stopped, shook hands, and

Mark gave a shove with his shoulder to the door which opened into cool emptiness.

'Why go home? The heck with it. Let's have a bite somewhere, you and I.' Adolf stood, propping himself on his cane as if it were a tail. 'The heck with it, Mark . . .'

Mark gave his cheek an irresolute rub, then laughed. 'All right. Only it's my treat.'

When, half an hour later, he came out of the pub and said goodbye to his friend, the flush of a fiery sunset filled the vista of the canal, and a rain-streaked bridge in the distance was margined by a narrow rim of gold along which passed tiny black figures.

He glanced at his watch and decided to go straight to his fiancée's without stopping at his mother's. His happiness and the limpidity of the evening air made his head spin a little. An arrow of bright copper struck the lacquered shoe of a fop jumping out of a car. The puddles, which still had not dried, surrounded by the bruise of dark damp (the live eyes of the asphalt), reflected the soft incandescence of the evening. The houses were as gray as ever; yet the roofs, the moldings above the upper floors, the gilt-edged lightning rods, the stone cupolas, the colonnettes – which nobody notices during the day, for day people seldom look up – were now bathed in rich ochre, the sunset's airy warmth, and thus they seemed unexpected and magical, those upper protrusions, balconies, cornices, pillars, contrasting sharply, because of their tawny brilliance, with the drab façades beneath.

Details of a Sunset

Oh, how happy I am, Mark kept musing, how everything around celebrates my happiness.

As he sat in the tram he tenderly, lovingly examined his fellow passengers. He had such a young face, had Mark, with pink pimples on the chin, glad luminous eyes, an untrimmed tag at the hollow of his nape . . . One would think fate might have spared him.

In a few moments I'll see Klara, he thought. She'll meet me at the door. She'll say she barely survived until evening.

He gave a start. He had missed the stop where he should have got off. On the way to the exit he tripped over the feet of a fat gentleman who was reading a medical journal; Mark wanted to tip his hat but nearly fell: the streetcar was turning with a screech. He grabbed an overhead strap and managed to keep his balance. The man slowly retracted his short legs with a phlegmy and cross growl. He had a gray mustache which twisted up pugnaciously. Mark gave him a guilty smile and reached the front end of the car. He grasped the iron hand-rails with both hands, leaned forward, calculated his jump. Down below, the asphalt streamed past, smooth and glistening. Mark jumped. There was a burn of friction against his soles, and his legs started running by themselves, his feet stamping with involuntary resonance. Several odd things occurred simultaneously: from the front of the car, as it swayed away from Mark, the conductor emitted a furious shout; the shiny asphalt swept upward like the seat of a swing; a roaring mass hit Mark from behind. He felt as if a thick thunderbolt had gone through him from head to toe, and then nothing. He was standing alone on the glossy asphalt. He looked around. He saw, at a distance, his own figure, the slender back of Mark Standfuss, who was walking diagonally across the street as if nothing had happened. Marveling, he caught up with himself in one easy sweep, and now it was he nearing the sidewalk, his entire frame filled with a gradually diminishing vibration.

That was stupid. Almost got run over by a bus . . .

The street was wide and gay. The colors of the sunset had invaded half of the sky. Upper stories and roofs were bathed in glorious light. Up there, Mark could discern translucent porticoes, friezes and frescoes, trellises covered with orange roses, winged statues that lifted skyward golden, unbearably blazing lyres. In bright undulations, ethereally, festively, these architectonic enchantments were receding into the heavenly distance, and Mark could not understand how he had never noticed before those galleries, those temples suspended on high.

He banged his knee painfully. That black fence again. He could not help laughing as he recognized the vans beyond. There they stood, like gigantic coffins. Whatever might they conceal within? Treasures? The skeletons of giants? Or dusty mountains of sumptuous furniture?

Oh, I must have a look. Or else Klara will ask, and I shan't know.

He gave a quick nudge to the door of one of the vans and went inside. Empty. Empty, except for one little straw chair in the center, comically poised askew on three legs.

Mark shrugged and went out on the opposite side. Once again the hot evening glow gushed into sight. And now in front of him was the familiar wrought-iron wicket, and further on Klara's window, crossed by a green branch. Klara herself opened the gate, and stood waiting, lifting her bared elbows, adjusting her hair. The russet tufts of her armpits showed through the sunlit openings of her short sleeves.

Mark, laughing noiselessly, ran up to embrace her. He pressed his cheek against the warm, green silk of her dress.

Her hands came to rest on his head.

'I was so lonely all day, Mark. But now you are here.'

She opened the door, and Mark immediately found himself in the dining room, which struck him as being inordinately spacious and bright.

'When people are as happy as we are now,' she said, 'they can do without a hallway,' Klara spoke in a passionate whisper, and he felt that her words had some special, wonderful meaning.

And in the dining room, around the snow-white oval of the tablecloth, sat a number of people, none of whom Mark had seen before at his fiancée's house. Among them was Adolf, swarthy, with his square-shaped head; there was also that short-legged, big-bellied old man who had been reading a medical journal in the tram and was still grumbling.

Mark greeted the company with a shy nod and sat

down beside Klara, and in that same instant felt, as he had a short time ago, a bolt of atrocious pain pass through his whole frame. He writhed, and Klara's green dress floated away, diminished, and turned into the green shade of a lamp. The lamp was swaying on its cord. Mark was lying beneath it, with that inconceivable pain crushing his body, and nothing could be distinguished save that oscillating lamp, and his ribs were pressing against his heart, making it impossible to breathe, and someone was bending his leg, straining to break it, in a moment it would crack. He freed himself somehow, the lamp glowed green again, and Mark saw himself sitting a little way off, beside Klara, and no sooner had he seen it than he found himself brushing his knee against her warm silk skirt. And Klara was laughing, her head thrown back.

He felt an urge to tell about what had just happened, and, addressing all those present – jolly Adolf, the irritable fat man – uttered with an effort: 'The foreigner is offering the aforementioned prayers on the river . . .'

It seemed to him that he had made everything clear, and apparently they had all understood . . . Klara, with a little pout, pinched his cheek: 'My poor darling. It'll be all right . . .'

He began to feel tired and sleepy. He put his arm around Klara's neck, drew her to him, and lay back. And then the pain pounced upon him again, and everything became clear.

Mark was lying supine, mutilated and bandaged, and the lamp was not swinging any longer. The familiar fat man with the mustache, now a doctor in a white gown, made worried growling small noises as he peered into the pupils of Mark's eyes. And what pain! . . . God, in a moment his heart would be impaled on a rib and burst . . . God, any instant now . . . This is silly. Why isn't Klara here? . . .

The doctor frowned and clucked his tongue.

Mark no longer breathed, Mark had departed – whither, into what other dreams, none can tell.

The Thunderstorm

At the corner of an otherwise ordinary West Berlin street, under the canopy of a linden in full bloom, I was enveloped by a fierce fragrance. Masses of mist were ascending in the night sky and, when the last star-filled hollow had been absorbed, the wind, a blind phantom, covering his face with his sleeves, swept low through the deserted street. In lusterless darkness, over the iron shutter of a barbershop, its suspended shield – a gilt shaving basin – began swinging like a pendulum.

I came home and found the wind waiting for me in the room: it banged the casement window – and staged a prompt reflux when I shut the door behind me. Under my window there was a deep courtyard where, in the daytime, shirts, crucified on sun-bright clotheslines, shone through the lilac bushes. Out of that yard voices would rise now and then: the melancholy barking of ragmen or empty-bottle buyers; sometimes, the wail of a crippled violin; and, once, an obese blonde woman stationed herself in the center of the yard and broke into such lovely song that maids leaned out of all the windows, bending their bare necks. Then, when she had finished, there was a moment of extraordinary stillness; only my landlady, a slatternly widow, was heard sobbing and blowing her nose in the corridor.

In that yard now a stifling gloom swelled, but then the blind wind, which had helplessly slithered into its depths, once again began reaching upward, and suddenly it regained its sight, swept up and, in the amber apertures of the black wall opposite, the silhouettes of arms and disheveled heads began to dart, as escaping windows were being caught and their frames resonantly and firmly locked. The lights went out. The next moment an avalanche of dull sound, the sound of distant thunder, came into motion, and started tumbling through the dark-violet sky. And again all grew still as it had when the beggar woman finished her song, her hands clasped to her ample bosom.

In this silence I fell asleep, exhausted by the happiness of my day, a happiness I cannot describe in writing, and my dream was full of you.

I woke up because the night had begun crashing to pieces. A wild, pale glitter was flying across the sky like a rapid reflection of colossal spokes. One crash after another rent the sky. The rain came down in a spacious and sonorous flow.

I was intoxicated by those bluish tremors, by the keen, volatile chill. I went up to the wet window ledge and inhaled the unearthly air, which made my heart ring like glass.

Ever nearer, ever more grandly, the prophet's chariot rumbled across the clouds. The light of madness, of piercing visions, illumined the nocturnal world,

The Thunderstorm

the metal slopes of roofs, the fleeing lilac bushes. The Thunder-god, a white-haired giant with a furious beard blown back over his shoulder by the wind, dressed in the flying folds of a dazzling raiment, stood, leaning backward, in his fiery chariot, restraining with tensed arms his tremendous, jet-black steeds, their manes a violet blaze. They had broken away from the driver's control, they scattered sparkles of crackling foam, the chariot careened, and the flustered prophet tugged at the reins in vain. His face was distorted by the blast and the strain; the whirlwind, blowing back the folds of his garment, bared a mighty knee; the steeds tossed their blazing manes and rushed on ever more violently, down, down along the clouds. Then, with thunderous hooves, they hurtled across a shiny rooftop, the chariot lurched, Elijah staggered, and the steeds, maddened by the touch of mortal metal, sprang skyward again. The prophet was pitched out. One wheel came off. From my window I saw its enormous fiery hoop roll down the roof, teeter at the edge, and jump off into darkness, while the steeds, dragging the overturned chariot, were already speeding along the highest clouds; the rumble died down, and the stormy blaze vanished in livid chasms.

The Thunder-god, who had fallen onto the roof, rose heavily. His sandals started slipping; he broke a dormer window with his foot, grunted, and, with a sweep of his arm grasped a chimney to steady himself. He slowly turned his frowning face as his eyes searched for something – probably the wheel that had flown off its golden axle. Then he glanced upward, his fingers clutching at his ruffled beard, shook his head crossly – this was probably not the first time that it happened – and, limping slightly, began a cautious descent.

In great excitement I tore myself away from the window, hurried to put on my dressing gown, and ran down the steep staircase straight to the courtyard. The storm had blown over but a waft of rain still lingered in the air. To the east an exquisite pallor was invading the sky.

The courtyard, which from above had seemed to brim with dense darkness, contained, in fact, nothing more than a delicate, melting mist. On its central patch of turf darkened by the damp, a lean, stoop-shouldered old man in a drenched robe stood muttering something and looking around him. Upon seeing me, he blinked angrily and said, 'That you, Elisha?'

I bowed. The prophet clucked his tongue, scratching the while his bald brown spot.

'Lost a wheel. Find it for me, will you?'

The rain had now ceased. Enormous flame-colored clouds collected above the roofs. The shrubs, the fence, the glistening kennel, were floating in the bluish, drowsy air around us. We groped for a long time in various corners. The old man kept grunting, hitching up the heavy hem of his robe, splashing through the puddles with his round-toed sandals, and a bright drop hung from the tip of his large, bony nose. As I brushed aside a low branch of lilac, I noticed, on a pile of rubbish, amid broken glass, a narrow-rimmed iron wheel that must have belonged to a baby carriage. The old man exhaled warm relief

The Thunderstorm

above my ear. Hastily, even a little brusquely, he pushed me aside, and snatched up the rusty hoop. With a joyful wink he said, 'So that's where it rolled.'

Then he stared at me, his white eyebrows came together in a frown, and, as if remembering something, he said in an impressive voice, 'Turn away, Elisha.'

I obeyed, even shutting my eyes. I stood like that for a minute or so, and then could not control my curiosity any longer.

The courtyard was empty, except for the old, shaggy dog with its graying muzzle that had thrust its head out of the kennel and was looking up, like a person, with frightened hazel eyes. I looked up too. Elijah had scrambled onto the roof, the iron hoop glimmering behind his back. Above the black chimneys a curly auroral cloud loomed like an orange-hued mountain and, beyond it, a second and a third. The hushed dog and I watched together as the prophet, who had reached the crest of the roof, calmly and unhurriedly stepped upon the cloud and continued to climb, treading heavily on masses of mellow fire . . .

Sunlight shot through his wheel whereupon it became at once huge and golden, and Elijah himself now seemed robed in flame, blending with the paradisal cloud along which he walked higher and higher until he disappeared in a glorious gorge of the sky.

Only then did the decrepit dog break into a hoarse morning bark. Ripples ran across the bright surface of a rain puddle. The light breeze stirred the geraniums on the balconies. Two or three windows awakened. In my soaked bedslippers and worn dressing gown I ran out into the street to overtake the first, sleepy tramcar, and pulling the skirts of my gown around me, and laughing to myself as I ran, I imagined how, in a few moments, I would be in your house and start telling you about that night's midair accident, and the cross old prophet who fell into my yard.

A Nursery Tale

1

Fantasy, the flutter, the rapture of fantasy! Erwin knew these things well. In a tram, he would always sit on the right-hand side, so as to be nearer the sidewalk. Twice daily, from the tram he took to the office and back, Erwin looked out of the window and collected his harem. Happy, happy Erwin, to dwell in such a convenient, such a fairy-tale German town!

He covered one sidewalk in the morning, on his way to work, and the other in the late afternoon, on his way home. First one, then the other was bathed in voluptuous sunlight, for the sun also went and returned. We should bear in mind that Erwin was so morbidly shy that only once in his life, taunted by rascally comrades, he had accosted a woman, and she had said quietly: 'You ought to be ashamed of yourself. Leave me alone.' Thereafter, he had avoided conversation with strange young ladies. In compensation, separated from the street by a windowpane, clutching to his ribs a black briefcase, wearing scuffed trousers with a pinstripe, and stretching one leg under the opposite seat (if unoccupied), Erwin looked boldly and freely at passing girls, and then would suddenly bite his nether lip: this signified the capture of a new concubine; whereupon he would set her aside, as it were, and his swift gaze, jumping like a compass needle, was already seeking out the next one. Those beauties were far from him, and therefore the sweetness of free choice could not be affected by sullen timidity. If, however, a girl happened to sit down across from him, and a certain twinge told him that she was pretty, he would retract his leg from under her seat with all the signs of a gruffness quite uncharacteristic of his young age – and could not bring himself to take stock of her: the bones of his forehead – right here, over the eyebrows – ached from shyness, as if an iron helmet were restricting his temples and preventing him from raising his eyes; and what a relief it was when she got up and went toward the exit. Then, feigning casual abstraction, he looked – shameless Erwin did look – following her receding back, swallowing whole her adorable nape and silk-hosed calves, and thus, after all, would he add her to his fabulous harem! The leg would again be stretched, again the bright sidewalk would flow past the window, and again, his thin pale nose with a noticeable depression at the tip directed streetward, Erwin would accumulate his slave girls. And this is fantasy, the flutter, the rapture of fantasy!

2

One Saturday, on a frivolous evening in May, Erwin was sitting at a sidewalk table. He watched the tripping throng of the avenue, now and then biting his lip with

A Nursery Tale

a quick incisor. The entire sky was tinged with pink and the streetlamps and shop-sign bulbs glowed with a kind of unearthly light in the gathering dusk. The first lilacs were being hawked by an anemic but pretty young girl. Rather fittingly the café phonograph was singing the Flower Aria from Faust.

A tall middle-aged lady in a charcoal tailor-made suit, heavily, yet not ungracefully, swinging her hips, made her way among the sidewalk tables. There was no vacant one. Finally, she put one hand in a glossy black glove upon the back of the empty chair opposite Erwin.

'May I?' queried her unsmiling eyes from under the short veil of her velvet hat.

'Yes, certainly,' answered Erwin, slightly rising and ducking. He was not awed by such solid-built women with thickly powdered, somewhat masculine jowls.

Down onto the table with a resolute thud went her oversize handbag. She ordered a cup of coffee and a wedge of apple tart. Her deep voice was somewhat hoarse but pleasant.

The vast sky, suffused with dull rose, grew darker. A tram screeched by, inundating the asphalt with the radiant tears of its lights. And short-skirted beauties walked by. Erwin's glance followed them.

I want this one, he thought, noticing his nether lip. And that one, too.

'I think it could be arranged,' said his vis-à-vis in the same calm husky tones in which she had addressed the waiter.

Erwin almost fell off his chair. The lady looked

intently at him, as she pulled off one glove to tackle her coffee. Her made-up eyes shone cold and hard, like showy false jewels. Dark pouches swelled under them, and – what seldom occurs in the case of women, even elderly women – hairs grew out of her feline-shaped nostrils. The shed glove revealed a big wrinkled hand with long, convex, beautiful fingernails.

'Don't be surprised,' she said with a wry smile. She muffled a yawn and added: 'In point of fact, I am the Devil.'

Shy, naive Erwin took this to be a figure of speech, but the lady, lowering her voice, continued as follows:

'Those who imagine me with horns and a thick tail are greatly mistaken. Only once did I appear in that shape, to some Byzantine imbecile, and I really don't know why it was such a damned success. I am born three or four times every two centuries. In the 1870s, some fifty years ago, I was buried, with picturesque honors and a great shedding of blood, on a hill above a cluster of African villages of which I had been ruler. My term there was a rest after more stringent incarnations. Now I am a German-born woman whose last husband – I had, I think, three in all – was of French extraction, a Professor Monde. In recent years I have driven several young men to suicide, caused a well-known artist to copy and multiply the picture of the Westminster Abbey on the pound note, incited a virtuous family man – But there is really nothing to brag about. This has been a pretty banal avatar, and I am fed up with it.'

She gobbled up her slice of tart and Erwin, mumbling

A Nursery Tale

something, reached for his hat, which had fallen under the table.

'No, don't go yet,' said Frau Monde, simultaneously beckoning the waiter. 'I am offering you something. I am offering you a harem. And if you are still skeptical of my power – See that old gentleman in tortoiseshell glasses crossing the street? Let's have him hit by a tram.'

Erwin, blinking, turned streetward. As the old man reached the tracks he took out his handkerchief and was about to sneeze into it. At the same instant, a tram flashed, screeched, and rolled past. From both sides of the avenue people rushed toward the tracks. The old gentleman, his glasses and handkerchief gone, was sitting on the asphalt. Someone helped him up. He stood, sheepishly shaking his head, brushing his coat sleeves with the palms of his hands, and wiggling one leg to test its condition.

'I said "hit by a tram," not "run over," which I might also have said,' remarked Frau Monde coolly, as she worked a thick cigarette into an enameled holder. 'In any case, this is an example.'

She blew two streams of gray smoke through her nostrils and again fixed Erwin with her hard bright eyes.

'I liked you immediately. That shyness, that bold imagination. You reminded me of an innocent, though hugely endowed, young monk whom I knew in Tuscany. This is my penultimate night. Being a woman has its points, but being an aging woman is hell, if you will pardon me the expression. Moreover, I made such mischief the other day – you will soon read about it in all the papers – that I had better get out of this life. Next Monday I plan to be born elsewhere. The Siberian slut I have chosen shall be the mother of a marvelous, monstrous man.'

'I see,' said Erwin.

'Well, my dear boy,' continued Frau Monde, demolishing her second piece of pastry, 'I intend, before going, to have a bit of innocent fun. Here is what I suggest. Tomorrow, from noon to midnight you can select by your usual method' (with heavy humor Frau Monde sucked in her lower lip with a succulent hiss) 'all the girls you fancy. Before my departure, I shall have them gathered and placed at your complete disposal. You will keep them until you have enjoyed them all. How does that strike you, *arnica!*'

Erwin dropped his eyes and said softly: 'If it is all true, it would be a great happiness.'

'All right then,' she said, and licked the remains of whipped cream off her spoon: 'All right. One condition, nevertheless, must be set. No, it is not what you are thinking. As I told you, I have arranged my next incarnation. *Your* soul I do not require. Now this is the condition: the total of your choices between noon and midnight must be an odd number. This is essential and final. Otherwise I can do nothing for you.'

Erwin cleared his throat and asked, almost in a whisper: 'But – how shall I know? Let's say I've chosen one – what then?'

'Nothing,' said Frau Monde. 'Your feeling, your desire, are a command in themselves. However, in order that

A Nursery Tale

you may be sure that the deal stands, I shall have a sign given you every time – a smile, not necessarily addressed to you, a chance word in the crowd, a sudden patch of color – that sort of thing. Don't worry, you'll know.'

'And – and—' mumbled Erwin, shuffling his feet under the table: '– and where is it all going to – uh – happen? I have only a very small room.'

'Don't worry about that either,' said Frau Monde, and her corset creaked as she rose. 'Now it's time you went home. No harm in getting a good night's rest. I'll give you a lift.'

In the open taxi, with the dark wind streaming between starry sky and glistening asphalt, poor Erwin felt tremendously elated. Frau Monde sat erect, her crossed legs forming a sharp angle, and the city lights flashed in her gemlike eyes.

'Here's your house,' she said, touching Erwin's shoulder. '*Au revoir.*'

3

Many are the dreams that can be brought on by a mug of dark beer laced with brandy. Thus reflected Erwin when he awoke the next morning – he must have been drunk, and the talk with that funny female was all fancy. This rhetorical turn often occurs in fairy tales and, as in fairy tales, our young man soon realized he was wrong.

He went out just as the church clock had begun the laborious task of striking noon. Sunday bells joined in excitedly, and a bright breeze ruffled the Persian lilacs around the public lavatory in the small park near his house. Pigeons settled on an old stone *Herzog* or waddled along the sandbox where little children, their flannel behinds sticking up, were digging with toy scoops and playing with wooden trains. The lustrous leaves of the lindens moved in the wind; their ace-of-spades shadows quivered on the graveled path and climbed in an airy flock the trouser legs and skirts of the strollers, racing up and scattering over shoulders and faces, and once again the whole flock slipped back onto the ground, where, barely stirring, they lay in wait for the next foot passenger. In this variegated setting, Erwin noticed a girl in a white dress who had squatted down to tousle with two fingers a fat shaggy pup with warts on its belly. The inclination of her head bared the back of her neck, revealing the ripple of her vertebrae, the fair bloom, the tender hollow between her shoulder blades, and the sun through the leaves found fiery strands in her chestnut hair. Still playing with the puppy, she half-rose from her haunches and clapped her hands above it. The fat little animal rolled over on the gravel, ran off a few feet, and toppled on its side. Erwin sat down on a bench and cast a timid and avid glance at her face.

He saw her so clearly, with such piercing and perfect force of perception, that, it seemed, nothing new about her features might have been disclosed by years of previous intimacy. Her palish lips twitched as if repeating every small soft movement of the puppy; her eyelashes beat so brightly as to look like the raylets of her beaming eyes; but most enchanting,

A Nursery Tale

perhaps, was the curve of her cheek, now slightly in profile; that dipping line no words, of course, could describe. She started running, showing nice legs, and the puppy tumbled in her wake like a woolly ball. In sudden awareness of his miraculous might, Erwin caught his breath and awaited the promised signal. At that moment the girl turned her head as she ran and flashed a smile at the plump little creature that could barely keep up with her.

'Number one,' Erwin said to himself with unwonted complacency, and got up from his bench.

He followed the graveled path with scraping footsteps, in gaudy, reddish-yellow shoes worn only on Sundays. He left the oasis of the diminutive park and crossed over to Amadeus Boulevard. Did his eyes rove? Oh, they did. But, maybe, because the girl in white had somehow left a sunnier mark than any remembered impression, some dancing blind spot prevented him from finding another sweetheart. Soon, however, the blot dissolved, and near a glazed pillar with the tramway timetable our friend observed two young ladies – sisters, or even twins, to judge by their striking resemblance – who were discussing a streetcar route in vibrant, echoing voices. Both were small and slim, dressed in black silk, with saucy eyes and painted lips.

'That's exactly the tram you want,' one of them kept saying.

'Both, please,' Erwin requested quickly.

'Yes, of course,' said the other in response to her sister's words.

Erwin continued along the boulevard. He knew all the smart streets where the best possibilities existed.

'Three,' he said to himself. 'Odd number. So far so good. And if it were midnight right now—'

Swinging her handbag she was coming down the steps of the Leilla, one of the best local hotels. Her big blue-chinned companion slowed down behind her to light his cigar. The lady was lovely, hatless, bobhaired, with a fringe on her forehead that made her look like a boy actor in the part of a damsel. As she went by, now closely escorted by our ridiculous rival, Erwin remarked simultaneously the crimson artificial rose in the lapel of her jacket and the advertisement on a billboard: a blond-mustachioed Turk and, in large letters, the word 'YES!,' under which it said in smaller characters: 'I SMOKE ONLY THE ROSE OF THE ORIENT.'

That made four, divisible by two, and Erwin felt eager to restore the odd-number rigmarole without delay. In a lane off the boulevard there was a cheap restaurant which he sometimes frequented on Sundays when sick of his landlady's fare. Among the girls he had happened to note at one time or another there had been a wench who worked in that place. He entered and ordered his favorite dish: blood sausage and sauerkraut. His table was next to the telephone. A man in a bowler called a number and started to jabber as ardently as a hound that has picked up the scent of a hare. Erwin's glance wandered toward the bar – and there was the girl he had seen three or four times before. She was beautiful in a drab, freckled way, if beauty can be drably russet. As she raised her bare arms to place her washed beer steins he saw the red tufts of her armpits.

'All right, all right!' barked the man into the mouthpiece.

With a sigh of relief enriched by a belch, Erwin left the restaurant. He felt heavy and in need of a nap. To tell the truth, the new shoes pinched like crabs. The weather had changed. The air was sultry. Great domed clouds grew and crowded one another in the hot sky. The streets were becoming deserted. One could feel the houses fill to the brim with Sunday-afternoon snores. Erwin boarded a streetcar.

The tram started to roll. Erwin turned his pale face, shining with sweat, to the window, but no girls walked. While paying his fare he noticed, on the other side of the aisle, a woman sitting with her back to him. She wore a black velvet hat, and a light frock patterned with intertwined chrysanthemums against a semitransparent mauve background through which showed the shoulder straps of her slip. The lady's statuesque bulk made Erwin curious to glimpse her face. When her hat moved and, like a black ship, started to turn, he first looked away as usual, glanced in feigned abstraction at a youth sitting opposite him, at his own fingernails, at a red-cheeked little old man dozing in the rear of the car, and, having thus established a point of departure justifying further castings-around, Erwin shifted his casual gaze to the lady now looking his way. It was Frau Monde. Her full, no-longer-young face was blotchily flushed from the heat, her mannish eyebrows bristled above her piercing prismatic eyes, a slightly sardonic smile curled up the corners of her compressed lips.

'Good afternoon,' she said in her soft husky voice: 'Come sit over here. Now we can have a chat. How are things going?'

'Only five,' replied Erwin with embarrassment.

'Excellent. An odd number. I would advise you to stop there. And at midnight – ah, yes, I don't think I told you – at midnight you are to come to Hoffmann Street. Know where that is? Look between Number Twelve and Fourteen. The vacant lot there will be replaced by a villa with a walled garden. The girls of your choice will be waiting for you on cushions and rugs. I shall meet you at the garden gate – but it is understood,' she added with a subtle smile, 'I shan't intrude. You'll remember the address? There will be a brand-new streetlight in front of the gate.'

'Oh, one thing,' said Erwin, collecting his courage. 'Let them be dressed at first – I mean let them look just as they were when I chose them – and let them be very merry and loving.'

'Why, naturally,' she replied, 'everything will be just as you wish whether you tell me or not. Otherwise there was no point in starting the whole business, *n' est-ce pas?* Confess, though, my dear boy – you were on the brink of enrolling me in your harem. No, no, have no fear, I am kidding you. Well, that's your stop. Very wise to call it a day. Five is fine. See you a few secs after midnight, ha-ha.'

4

Upon reaching his room, Erwin took off his shoes and stretched out on the bed. He woke up toward evening. A mellifluous tenor at full blast streamed from a neighbor's phonograph: *'I vant to be happee—'*

Erwin started thinking back: Number one, the Maiden in White, she's the most artless of the lot. I may have been a little hasty. Oh, well, no harm done. Then the Twins near the pillar of glass. Gay, painted young things. With them I'm sure to have fun. Then number four, Leilla the Rose, resembling a boy. That's, perhaps, the best one. And finally, the Fox in the ale-house. Not bad either. But only five. That's not very many!

He lay prone for a while with his hands behind his head, listening to the tenor, who kept wanting to be happy: Five. No, that's absurd. Pity it's not Monday morning: those three shopgirls the other day – oh, there are so many more beauties waiting to be found! And I can always throw in a streetwalker at the last moment.

Erwin put on his regular pair of shoes, brushed his hair, and hurried out.

By nine o'clock he had collected two more. One of them he noticed in a café where he had a sandwich and two drams of Dutch gin. She was talking with great animation to her companion, a beard-fingering foreigner, in an impenetrable language – Polish or Russian – and her gray eyes had a slight slant, her thin aquiline nose wrinkled when she laughed, and her elegant legs were exposed to the knee. While Erwin watched her quick gestures, the reckless way in which she tap-tapped cigarette ash all over the table, a German word, like a window, flashed open in her Slavic speech, and this chance word ('*offenbar*') was the 'evident' sign. The other girl, number seven on the list, turned up at the Chinese-style entrance of a small amusement park. She wore a scarlet blouse with a bright-green skirt, and her bare neck swelled as she shrieked in glee, fighting off a couple of slap-happy young boors who were grabbing her by the hips and trying to make her accompany them.

'I'm willing, I'm willing!' she cried out at last, and was rushed away.

Varicolored paper lanterns enlivened the place. A sledgelike affair with wailing passengers hurtled down a serpentine channel, disappeared in the angled arcades of medieval scenery, and dived into a new abyss with new howls. Inside a shed, on four bicycle seats (there were no wheels, just the frames, pedals, and handlebars), sat four girls in jerseys and shorts – a red one, a blue one, a green one, a yellow one – their bare legs working at full tilt. Above them hung a dial on which moved four pointers, red, blue, green, and yellow. At first the blue one was first, then the green overtook it. A man with a whistle stood by and collected the coins of the few simpletons who wanted to place their bets. Erwin stared at those magnificent legs, naked nearly up to the groin and pedaling with passionate power.

They must be terrific dancers, he thought; I could use all four.

A Nursery Tale

The pointers obediently gathered into one bunch and came to a stop.

'Dead heat!' shouted the man with the whistle. 'A sensational finish!'

Erwin drank a glass of lemonade, consulted his watch, and made for the exit.

Eleven o'clock and eleven women. That will do, I suppose.

He narrowed his eyes as he imagined the pleasures awaiting him. He was glad he had remembered to put on clean underwear.

How slyly Frau Monde put it, reflected Erwin with a smile. Of course she will spy on me and why not? It will add some spice.

He walked, looking down, shaking his head delightedly, and only rarely glancing up to check the street names. Hoffmann Street, he knew, was quite far, but he still had an hour, so there was no need to hurry. Again, as on the previous night, the sky swarmed with stars and the asphalt glistened like smooth water, absorbing and lengthening the magic lights of the town. He passed a large cinema whose radiance flooded the sidewalk, and at the next corner a short peal of childish laughter caused him to raise his eyes.

He saw before him a tall elderly man in evening clothes with a little girl walking beside – a child of fourteen or so in a low-cut black party dress. The whole city knew the elderly man from his portraits. He was a famous poet, a senile swan, living all alone in a distant suburb. He strode with a kind of ponderous grace;

his hair, the hue of soiled cotton wool, reached over his ears from beneath his fedora. A stud in the triangle of his starched shirt caught the gleam of a lamp, and his long bony nose cast a wedge of shadow on one side of his thin-lipped mouth. In the same tremulous instant Erwin's glance lit on the face of the child mincing at the old poet's side; there was something odd about that face, odd was the flitting glance of her much too shiny eyes, and if she were not just a little girl – the old man's granddaughter, no doubt – one might suspect that her lips were touched up with rouge. She walked swinging her hips very, very slightly, her legs moved closer together, she was asking her companion something in a ringing voice – and although Erwin gave no command mentally, he knew that his swift secret wish had been fulfilled.

'Oh, of course, of course,' replied the old man coaxingly, bending toward the child.

They passed, Erwin caught a whiff of perfume. He looked back, then went on.

'Hey, careful,' he suddenly muttered as it dawned upon him that this made twelve – an even number: I must find one more – within half an hour.

It vexed him a little to go on searching, but at the same time he was pleased to be given yet another chance.

I'll pick up one on the way, he said to himself, allaying a trace of panic. I'm sure to find one!

'Maybe, it will be the nicest of all,' he remarked aloud as he peered into the glossy night.

And a few minutes later he experienced the familiar delicious contraction – that chill in the solar plexus. A

A Nursery Tale

woman in front of him was walking along with rapid and light steps. He saw her only from the back and could not have explained why he yearned so poignantly to overtake precisely *her* and have a look at her face. One might, naturally, find random words to describe her bearing, the movement of her shoulders, the silhouette of her hat – but what is the use? Something beyond visible outlines, some kind of special atmosphere, an ethereal excitement, lured Erwin on and on. He marched fast and still could not catch up with her; the humid reflections of lights flickered before him; she tripped along steadily, and her black shadow would sweep up, as it entered a streetlamp's aura, glide across a wall, twist around its edge, and vanish.

'Goodness, I've got to see her face,' Erwin muttered. 'And time is flying.'

Presently he forgot about time. That strange silent chase in the night intoxicated him. He managed at last to overtake her and went on, far ahead, but had not the courage to look back at her and merely slowed down, whereupon she passed him in her turn and so fast that he did not have time to raise his eyes. Again he was walking ten paces behind her and by then he knew, without seeing her face, that she was his main prize. Streets burst into colored light, petered out, glowed again; a square had to be crossed, a space of sleek blackness, and once more with a brief click of her high-heeled shoe the woman stepped onto a sidewalk, with Erwin behind, bewildered, disembodied, dizzy from the misty lights, the damp night, the chase.

What enticed him? Not her gait, not her shape, but something else, bewitching and overwhelming, as if a tense shimmer surrounded her: mere fantasy, maybe, the flutter, the rapture of fantasy, or maybe it was that which changes a man's entire life with one divine stroke – Erwin knew nothing, he just sped after her over asphalt and stone, which seemed also dematerialized in the iridescent night.

Then trees, vernal lindens, joined the hunt: they advanced whispering on either side, overhead, all around him; the little black hearts of their shadows intermingled at the foot of each streetlamp, and their delicate sticky aroma encouraged him.

Once again Erwin came near. One more step, and he would be abreast of her. She stopped abruptly at an iron wicket and fished out her keys from her handbag. Erwin's momentum almost made him bump into her. She turned her face toward him, and by the light a streetlamp cast through emerald leaves, he recognized the girl who had been playing that morning with a woolly black pup on a graveled path, and immediately remembered, immediately understood all her charm, tender warmth, priceless radiance.

He stood staring at her with a wretched smile.

'You ought to be ashamed of yourself,' she said quietly. 'Leave me alone.'

The little gate opened, and slammed. Erwin remained standing under the hushed lindens. He looked around, not knowing which way to go. A few paces away, he saw two blazing bubbles: a car standing by the sidewalk. He went up to it and touched the motionless, dummylike chauffeur on the shoulder.

'Tell me what street is this? I'm lost.'

'Hoffmann Street,' said the dummy dryly.

And then a familiar, husky, soft voice spoke out of the depths of the car.

'Hello. It's me.'

Erwin leaned a hand on the car door and limply responded.

'I am bored to death,' said the voice, 'I'm waiting here for my boyfriend. He is bringing the poison. He and I are dying at dawn. How are you?'

'Even number,' said Erwin, running his finger along the dusty door.

'Yes, I know,' calmly rejoined Frau Monde. 'Number thirteen turned out to be number one. You bungled the job rather badly.'

'A pity,' said Erwin.

'A pity,' she echoed, and yawned.

Erwin bowed, kissed her large black glove, stuffed with five outspread fingers, and with a little cough turned into the darkness. He walked with a heavy step, his legs ached, he was oppressed by the thought that tomorrow was Monday and it would be hard to get up.

Easter Rain

That day a lonely old Swiss woman named Joséphine, or Josefina Lvovna, as the Russian family she had once lived with for twelve years had dubbed her, bought half a dozen eggs, a black brush, and two buttons of carmine watercolor. That day the apple trees were in bloom. A cinema poster on the corner was reflected upside down on the smooth surface of a puddle, and, in the morning, the mountains on the far side of Lake Léman were all veiled in silky mist, like the opaque sheets of rice paper that cover etchings in expensive books. The mist promised a fair day, but the sun barely skimmed over the roofs of the skewed little stone houses, over the wet wires of a toy tram, and then dissolved once again into the haze. The day turned out to be calm, with springtime clouds, but, toward evening, a weighty, icy wind wafted down from the mountains, and Joséphine, on her way home, broke into such a fit of coughing that she lost her balance for a moment by the door, flushed crimson, and leaned on her tightly furled umbrella, thin as a black walking stick.

It was already dark in her room. When she turned on the lamp, it illuminated her hands – thin hands with tight, glossy skin, ecchymotic freckles, and white blotches on the fingernails.

Joséphine laid out her purchases on the table and dropped her coat and hat on the bed. She poured some water into a glass and, putting on a black-rimmed pince-nez that made her dark gray eyes look stern beneath the thick funereal brows that grew together over the bridge of her nose, began painting the eggs. For some reason the carmine watercolor would not stick. Perhaps she should have bought some kind of chemical paint, but she did not know how to ask for it, and was too embarrassed to explain. She thought about going to see a pharmacist she knew – while she was at it, she could get some aspirin. She felt so sluggish, and her eyeballs ached with fever. She wanted to sit quietly, think quietly. Today was the Russian Holy Saturday.

At one time, the peddlers on the Nevsky Prospect had sold a special kind of tongs. These tongs were very practical for fishing out the eggs from the hot, dark blue or orange liquid. But there were also the wooden spoons: They would bump lightly and compactly against the thick glass of the jars from which rose the heady steam of the dye. The eggs were then dried in piles, the red with the red, the green with the green. And they used to color them another way too, by wrapping them tightly in strips of cloth with decalcomanias tucked inside that looked like samples of wallpaper. After the boiling, when the man-servant brought the huge pot back from the kitchen, what fun it was to unravel the cloth and take the speckled, marbled eggs out of the warm, damp fabric, from which rose gentle steam, a whiff of one's childhood.

Easter Rain

The old Swiss woman felt strange remembering that, when she lived in Russia, she had been homesick, and sent long, melancholy, beautifully written letters to her friends back home about how she always felt unwanted, misunderstood. Every morning after breakfast she would go for a ride in the large open landau with her charge, Hélène. And next to the coachman's fat bottom, reminiscent of a gigantic blue pumpkin, was the hunched-over back of the old footman, all gold buttons and cockade. The only Russian words she knew were: 'Coachman,' 'good,' 'fine' [*kutcher, tish-tish, nichevo (coachman, hush-hush, so-so,* all mispronounced)].

She had left Petersburg with a dim sense of relief, just as the war was beginning. She thought that now she would delight endlessly in chatty evenings with her friends and in the coziness of her native town. But the reality turned out to be quite the opposite. Her real life – in other words, the part of life when one most keenly and deeply gets used to people and things – had passed by there, in Russia, which she had unconsciously grown to love and understand, and where God only knew what was going on now . . . And tomorrow was Orthodox Easter.

Joséphine sighed loudly, got up, and closed the window more firmly. She looked at her watch, black on its nickel chain. She would have to do something about those eggs. They were to be a gift for the Platonovs, an elderly Russian couple recently settled in Lausanne, a town both native and foreign to her, where it was hard to breathe, where the houses were stacked at random, in disorder, helter-skelter, along the steep, angular streets.

She grew pensive, listening to the drone in her ears. Then she shook herself out of her torpor, poured a vial of purple ink into a tin can, and carefully lowered an egg into it.

The door opened softly. Her neighbor Mademoiselle Finard entered, quiet as a mouse. She was a thin little woman, a former governess herself. Her short-cropped hair was all silver. She was draped in a black shawl, iridescent with glass beads.

Joséphine, hearing her mouselike steps, awkwardly, with a newspaper, covered the can and the eggs that were drying on some blotting paper.

'What do you want? I don't like people simply coming in like that.'

Mademoiselle Finard looked askance at Joséphine's anxious face and said nothing, but was deeply offended, and, without a word, left the room with the same mincing steps.

By now the eggs had turned a venomous violet. On an unpainted egg, she decided to draw the two Easter initials,* as had always been customary in Russia. The first letter, 'X', she drew well, but the second she could not quite remember, and finally, instead of a 'B', she drew an absurd, crooked 'R'. When the ink had dried completely

---

* The Cyrillic letters X (Kh) and B (V) stand for *Khristos vorkresye*, 'Christ has risen.'

Easter Rain

she wrapped the eggs in soft toilet paper and put them in her leather handbag.

But what tormenting sluggishness . . . She wanted to lie down in bed, drink some hot coffee, and stretch out her legs . . . She was feverish and her eyelids prickled . . . When she went outside, the dry crackle of her cough began rising in her throat again. The streets were dark, damp, and deserted. The Platonovs lived nearby. They were seated, having tea, and Platonov, bald-pated, with a scanty beard, in a Russian serge shirt with buttons on the side, was stuffing yellow tobacco into cigarette papers when Joséphine knocked with the knob of her umbrella and entered.

'Ah, good evening, Mademoiselle.'

She sat down next to them, and tactlessly, verbosely started discussing the imminent Russian Easter. She took the violet eggs out of her bag one by one. Platonov noticed the egg with the lilac letters 'X R' and burst out laughing.

'Whatever made her stick on those Jewish initials?'

His wife, a plump woman with a yellow wig and sorrowful eyes, smiled fleetingly. She started thanking Joséphine with indifference, drawing out her French vowels. Joséphine did not understand why they were laughing. She felt hot and sad. She began talking again, but she had the feeling that what she was saying was out of place, yet she could not restrain herself.

'Yes, at this moment there is no Easter in Russia . . . Poor Russia! Oh, I remember how people used to kiss each other in the streets. And my little Hélène looked like an angel that day . . . Oh, I often cry all night thinking of your wonderful country!'

The Platonovs always found these conversations unpleasant. They never discussed their lost homeland with outsiders, just as ruined rich men hide their poverty and become even haughtier and less approachable than before. Therefore, deep down, Joséphine felt that they had no love at all for Russia. Usually when she visited the Platonovs she thought that, if she only began talking of beautiful Russia with tears in her eyes, the Platonovs would suddenly burst into sobs and begin reminiscing and recounting, and that the three of them would sit like that all night reminiscing, crying, and squeezing each other's hands.

But in reality this never happened. Platonov would nod politely and indifferently with his beard, while his wife kept trying to find out where one could get some tea or soap as cheaply as possible.

Platonov began rolling his cigarettes again. His wife placed them evenly in a cardboard box. They had both intended to take a nap until it was time to leave for the Easter Vigils at the Greek church around the corner. They wanted to sit silently, to think their own thoughts, to speak only with glances and special, seemingly absentminded smiles about their son, who had been killed in the Crimea, about Easter odds and ends, about their neighborhood church on Pochtamskaya Street. Now this chattering, sentimental old woman with her anxious dark gray eyes had come, full of sighs, and might well stay until they left the house themselves.

Easter Rain

Joséphine fell silent, hoping avidly that she too might be asked to accompany them to church, and, afterward, to breakfast with them. She knew they had baked Russian Easter cakes the day before, and although she obviously could not eat any because she felt so feverish, still it would have been so pleasant, so warm, and so festive.

Platonov ground his teeth and, stifling a yawn, looked furtively at his wrist, at the dial under its little screen. Joséphine saw they were not going to invite her. She rose.

'You need a small rest, my dear friends, but there is something I want to say to you before I leave.' And, moving close to Platonov, who also got up, she exclaimed in sonorous, fractured Russian, 'Hath Christs rised!'

This was her last hope of eliciting a burst of hot, sweet tears, Easter kisses, an invitation to breakfast together . . . But Platonov only squared his shoulders and said with a subdued laugh, 'See, Mademoiselle, you pronounce Russian beautifully.'

Once outside, she broke into sobs, and walked pressing her handkerchief to her eyes, swaying slightly, tapping her silken, canelike umbrella on the sidewalk. The sky was cavernous and troubled – the moon vague, the clouds like ruins. The angled feet of a curly-headed Chaplin were reflected in a puddle near a brightly lit cinema. And when Joséphine walked beneath the noisy, weeping trees beside the lake, which seemed like a wall of mist, she saw an emerald lantern glowing faintly at the edge of a small pier and something large and white clambering onto a black boat that bobbed below. She focused through her tears. An enormous old swan puffed itself up, flapped its wings, and suddenly, clumsy as a goose, waddled heavily onto the deck. The boat rocked; green circles welled over the black, oily water that merged into fog.

Joséphine pondered whether she should perhaps go to church anyway. But in Petersburg the only church she had ever gone to was the red Catholic one at the end of Morskaya Street, and she felt ashamed now to go into an Orthodox church, where she did not know when to cross herself or how one held one's fingers, and where somebody might make a comment. She felt intermittent chills. Her head filled with a confusion of rustling, of smacking trees, of black clouds, and Easter recollections: mountains of multicolored eggs, the dusky sheen of St Isaac's. Deafened and woozy, she somehow managed to make it home and climb the stairs, banging her shoulder against the wall, and then, unsteadily, her teeth chattering, she began undressing. She felt weaker, and tumbled onto her bed with a blissful, incredulous smile.

A delirium, stormy and powerful as the surge of bells, took hold of her. Mountains of multicolored eggs scattered with rotund tapping sounds. The sun – or was it a golden-horned sheep made of creamery butter? – came tumbling through the window and began to grow, filling the room with torrid yellow. Meanwhile, the eggs scurried up and roiled down glossy little strips of wood, knocking against each other, their shells cracking, their whites streaked with crimson.

Easter Rain

All night she lay delirious like that, and it was only the following morning that a still-offended Mademoiselle Finard came in, gasped, and ran off in panic to call a doctor.

'Lobar pneumonia, Mademoiselle.'

Through the waves of delirium twinkled wallpaper flowers, the old woman's silver hair, the doctor's placid eyes – it all twinkled and dissolved. And again an agitated drone of joy engulfed her soul. The fable-blue sky was like a gigantic painted egg, bells thundered, and someone came into the room who looked like Platonov, or maybe like Hélène's father – and on entering he unfolded a newspaper, placed it on the table, and sat down nearby, glancing now at Joséphine, now at the white pages with a significant, modest, slightly cunning smile. Joséphine knew that in this paper there was some kind of wondrous news, but, try as she might, she could not decipher the Russian letters of the black headline. Her guest kept smiling and casting significant glances at her, and seemed on the very point of revealing the secret, to confirm the happiness that she foretasted – but the man slowly dissolved. Unconsciousness swept over her like a black cloud.

Then came another motley of delirious dreams: The landau rolled along the quay, Hélène lapped the hot bright color from a wooden spoon, the broad Neva sparkled expansively, and Czar Peter suddenly leapt off his bronze steed, the hooves of both its forelegs having simultaneously alighted. He approached Joséphine, and, with a smile on his green-tinted, stormy face, embraced her, kissed her on one cheek, then on the other. His lips were soft and warm, and when he brushed her cheek for the third time, she palpitated, moaning with bliss, spread out her arms, and silently fell silent.

Early in the morning, on the sixth day of her illness, after a final crisis, Joséphine came to her senses. A white sky shimmered brightly through the window and perpendicular rain was rustling and rippling in the gutters.

A wet branch stretched across the windowpane, and at its very end a leaf kept shuddering beneath the patter of the rain. The leaf leaned forward and let a large drop fall from the tip of its green blade. The leaf shuddered again, and again a moist ray rolled downward then a long, bright earring dangled and dropped.

And it seemed to Joséphine as if the rainy coolness were flowing through her veins. She could not take her eyes off the streaming sky, and the pulsating, enraptured rain was so pleasant, the leaf shuddered so touchingly, that she wanted to laugh; the laughter filled her, though it was still soundless, coursing through her body, tickling her palate, and was on the very point of erupting.

To her left, in the corner, something scrabbled and sighed. Aquiver with the laughter that was mounting in her, she took her eyes off the window and turned her head. The little old woman lay facedown on the floor in her black kerchief. Her short-cropped silver hair shook angrily as she fidgeted, thrusting her hand under the chest of drawers, where her ball of wool had rolled. Black yarn stretched from the chest to the chair, where her knitting needles and a half-knitted stocking still lay.

Easter Rain

Seeing Mademoiselle Finard's black hair, her squirming legs, her button boots, Joséphine broke out in peals of laughter, shaking as she gasped and cooed beneath her down comforter, feeling that she was resurrected, that she had returned from faraway mists of happiness, wonder, and Easter splendor.

The Dragon

He lived in reclusion in a deep, murky cave, in the very heart of a rocky mountain, feeding only on bats, rats, and mold. Occasionally, it is true, stalactite hunters or snoopy travelers would come peeking into the cave, and that was a tasty treat. Other pleasant memories included a brigand attempting to flee from justice, and two dogs that were once let loose to ascertain if the passage did not go clear through the mountain. The surrounding country was wild, porous snow lay here and there on the rock, and waterfalls rumbled with an icy roar. He had hatched some thousand years ago, and, perhaps because it had happened rather unexpectedly – the enormous egg was cracked open by a lightning bolt one stormy night – the dragon had turned out cowardly and not overly bright. Besides, he was strongly affected by his mother's death . . . She had long terrorized the neighboring villages, had spat flames, and the king would get cross, and around her lair incessantly prowled knights, whom she would crunch to pieces like walnuts. But once, when she had swallowed a plump royal chef and dozed off on a sun-warmed rock, the great Ganon himself galloped up in iron armor, on a black steed under silver netting. The poor sleepy thing went rearing up, her green and red humps flashing like bonfires, and the charging knight thrust his swift lance into her smooth white breast. She crashed to the ground, and promptly, out of the pink wound, sidled the corpulent chef with her enormous, steaming heart under his arm.

The young dragon saw all this from a hiding place behind the rock and, forever after, could not think about knights without a shudder. He withdrew into the depths of a cave, whence he never emerged. Thus passed ten centuries, equivalent to twenty dragon years.

Then, suddenly, he fell prey to unbearable melancholy . . . In fact, the spoiled food from the cave was provoking ferocious gastric alarms, revolting rumblings, and pain. He spent nine years making up his mind, and on the tenth, he did. Slowly and cautiously, gathering in and extending the rings of his tail, he clambered out of his cave.

Immediately he sensed that it was spring. The black rocks, washed by a recent downpour, were ashimmer; the sunlight boiled in the overflowing mountain torrent; the air was redolent of wild game. And the dragon, broadly inflating his flaming nostrils, started his descent into the valley. His satiny belly, white as a water lily, nearly touched the ground, crimson blotches stood out on his bloated green flanks, and the sturdy scales merged, on his back, into a jagged conflagration, a ridge of double ruddy humps, diminishing in size toward the potently, flexibly twitching tail. His head was smooth and greenish, bubbles of fiery mucus hung from his soft, warty underlip, and his giant, scaly paws left deep tracks, star-shaped concavities.

The Dragon

The first thing he saw upon descending into the valley was a railroad train traveling along rocky slopes. The dragon's first reaction was delight, since he mistook the train for a relative he could play with. Moreover, he thought that beneath that shiny, hard-looking shell there must surely be some tender meat. So he set off in pursuit, his feet slapping with a hollow, damp noise, but, just as he was about to gobble up the last car, the train sped into a tunnel. The dragon stopped, thrust his head into the black lair into which his quarry had vanished, but there was no way he could get in there. He dispatched a couple of torrid sneezes into the depths, then retracted his head, sat on his haunches, and began waiting – who knows, it might come running out again. After waiting some time he shook his head and moved on. At that instant a train did come scurrying out of the dark lair, gave a sly flash of window glass, and disappeared behind a curve. The dragon gave a hurt look over his shoulder and, raising his tail like a plume, resumed his journey.

Dusk was falling. Fog floated above the meadows. The gigantic beast, big as a live mountain, was seen by some homeward-bound peasants, who remained petrified with awe. A little auto speeding along the highway had all four of its tires blow out from fright, bounced, and ended up in the ditch. But the dragon walked on, noticing nothing; from afar came the hot scent of concentrated crowds of humans, and that is where he was headed. And, against the blue expanse of the night sky, there loomed before him black factory smokestacks, guardians of a large industrial town.

The main personages of this town were two: the owner of the Miracle Tobacco Company and that of the Big Helmet Tobacco Company. Between them raged age-old, subtle hostilities, about which one could write an entire epic poem. They were rivals in everything – the motley colors of their advertisements, their distribution techniques, pricing, and labor relations – but no one could say which had the upper hand. That memorable night, the owner of the Miracle Company stayed very late at his office. Nearby on his desk lay a stack of new, freshly printed advertisements that workmen from the co-operative were to plaster around the city at daybreak.

Suddenly a bell pierced the silence of the night and, a few moments later, entered a pale, haggard man with a burdocklike wart on his right cheek. The factory owner knew him: he was the proprietor of a model tavern the Miracle Company had set up on the outskirts.

'It's going on two in the morning, my friend. The only justification I can find for your visit is an event of unheard-of importance.'

'That's exactly the case,' said the tavern keeper in a calm voice, although his wart was twitching. This is what he reported:

He was bundling off five thoroughly soused old laborers. They must have seen something highly curious outdoors, for they all broke out laughing – 'Oh-ho-ho,' rumbled one of the voices, 'I must have had one glass too many, if I see, big as life, the hydra of counterrevo—'

He did not have time to finish, for there was a surge of terrifying, ponderous noise, and someone screamed.

The Dragon

The tavern keeper stepped outside to have a look. A monster, glimmering in the murk like a moist mountain, was swallowing something large with its head thrown back, which made its whitish neck swell with alternating hillocks; it swallowed and licked its chops, its whole body rocked, and it gently lay down in the middle of the street.

'I think it must have dozed off,' finished the tavern keeper, restraining the twitching wart with his finger.

The factory owner got up. The robust fillings of his teeth flashed with the golden fire of inspiration. The arrival of a live dragon aroused in him no other feelings than the passionate desire that guided him in every instance – the desire to inflict a defeat on the rival firm.

'Eureka,' he exclaimed. 'Listen, my good man, are there any other witnesses?'

'I don't think so,' the other replied. 'Everybody was in bed, and I decided not to wake anyone and came straight to you. So as to avoid panic.'

The factory owner donned his hat.

'Splendid. Take this – no, not the whole pile, thirty or forty sheets will do – and bring along this can, and the brush too. There, now show me the way.'

They went out into the dark night and were soon at the quiet street at the end of which, according to the tavern keeper, reposed a monster. First, by the light of a lone, yellow streetlamp, they saw a policeman standing on his head in the middle of the pavement. It turned out later that, while making his nightly rounds, he had come upon the dragon and had such a fright that he turned upside down and remained petrified in that attitude. The factory owner, a man with the size and strength of a gorilla, turned him right side up and leaned him against the lightpost; then he approached the dragon. The dragon was asleep, and no wonder. The individuals he had devoured, it so happened, were totally impregnated with wine, and had popped succulently between his jaws. The alcohol on an empty stomach had gone straight to his head and he had lowered the pellicles of his eyelids with a blissful smile. He lay on his belly with his front paws folded under, and the glow of the streetlamp highlighted the glistening arcs of the double vertebral protuberances.

'Set up the ladder,' said the factory owner. 'I'll do the pasting myself.'

And, choosing flat spots on the slimy green flanks of the monster, he began unhurriedly brushing paste on the scaly skin and affixing ample advertising posters. When he had used all the sheets, he gave the brave tavern keeper a meaningful handshake and, chomping on his cigar, returned home.

Morning came, a magnificent spring morning softened by a lilac haze. And suddenly the street came alive with a merry, excited din, doors and windows slammed, people poured into the street, mingling with those who were hurrying somewhere, laughing as they went. What they saw was a perfectly lifelike dragon, all covered with colorful advertisements, slapping listlessly along the asphalt. One poster was even stuck to the bald crown of his head, 'SMOKE ONLY MIRACLE BRAND,' rollicked the

The Dragon

blue and crimson letters of the ads. 'ONLY FOOLS DON'T SMOKE MY CIGARETTES,' 'MIRACLE TOBACCO TURNS AIR INTO HONEY,' 'MIRACLE, MIRACLE, MIRACLE!'

It really is a miracle, laughed the crowd, and how is it done – is it a machine or are there people inside?

The dragon was feeling rotten after his involuntary binge. The cheap wine now made him sick to his stomach, his whole body felt weak, and the thought of breakfast was out of the question. Besides, he was now overcome by an acute sense of shame, the excruciating shyness of a creature that finds itself amid a crowd for the first time. Frankly speaking, he very much wished to return as soon as possible to his cave, but that would have been even more shameful – therefore, he continued his grim progress through the town. Several men with placards on their backs protected him from the curious and from urchins who wanted to slip under his white belly, clamber onto his lofty backbone, or touch his snout. Music played, people gaped from every window, behind the dragon automobiles drove single file, and in one of them slouched the factory owner, the hero of the day.

The dragon walked without looking at anybody, dismayed by the incomprehensible merriment that he aroused.

Meanwhile, in a sunlit office, along a carpet soft as moss, paced to and fro with clenched fists the rival manufacturer, owner of the Big Helmet Company. At an open window, observing the procession, stood his girlfriend, a diminutive tightrope dancer.

'This is an outrage,' croaked over and again the manufacturer, a middle-aged, bald man with blue-gray bags of flabby skin under his eyes. 'The police ought to put a stop to this scandal . . . When did he manage to cobble together this stuffed dummy?'

'Ralph,' the dancer suddenly cried, clapping her hands. 'I know what you should do. We have a number at the circus called The Joust, and—'

In a torrid whisper, goggling her doll-like, mascara-lined eyes, she told him her plan. The manufacturer beamed. An instant later he was already on the phone with the circus manager.

'So,' said the manufacturer, hanging up. 'The dummy is made of inflated rubber. We'll see what's left of it if we give it a good prick.'

Meanwhile the dragon had crossed the bridge, passed the marketplace and the Gothic cathedral, which aroused some pretty repugnant memories, continued along the main boulevard, and was traversing a broad square when, parting the crowd, a knight unexpectedly came charging at him. The knight wore iron armor, visor lowered, a funereal plume on his helmet, and rode a ponderous black horse in silvery netting. Arms bearers – women dressed as pages – walked alongside, carrying picturesque, hastily devised banners heralding 'BIG HELMET,' 'SMOKE ONLY BIG HELMET,' 'BIG HELMET BEATS THEM ALL.' The circus rider impersonating the knight spurred his steed and clenched his lance. But the steed for some reason started backing, spurting foam, then suddenly reared up and sat heavily on its haunches.

The Dragon

The knight tumbled to the asphalt, with such a clatter one might think someone had thrown all the dishes out the window. But the dragon did not see this. At the knight's first move he had stopped abruptly, then rapidly turned, knocking down a pair of curious old women standing on a balcony with his tail as he did so, and, squashing the scattering spectators, had taken flight. He was out of the town in a single bound, flew across the fields, scrambled up the rocky slopes, and dove into his bottomless cavern. There he collapsed onto his back, paws folded and showing his satiny, white, shuddering belly to the dark vaults, heaved a deep breath, closed his astonished eyes, and died.

Revenge

I

Ostend, the stone wharf, the gray strand, the distant row of hotels, were all slowly rotating as they receded into the turquoise haze of an autumn day.

The professor wrapped his legs in a tartan lap robe, and the chaise longue creaked as he reclined into its canvas comfort. The clean, ochrered deck was crowded but quiet. The boilers heaved discreetly.

An English girl in worsted stockings, indicating the professor with a motion of her eyebrow, addressed her brother who was standing nearby: 'Looks like Sheldon, doesn't he?'

Sheldon was a comic actor, a bald giant with a round, flabby face. 'He's really enjoying the sea,' the girl added sotto voce. Whereupon, I regret to say, she drops out of my story.

Her brother, an ungainly, red-haired student on his way back to his university after the summer holidays, took the pipe out of his mouth and said, 'He's our biology professor. Capital old chap. Must say hello to him.' He approached the professor, who, lifting his heavy eyelids, recognized one of the worst and most diligent of his pupils.

'Ought to be a splendid crossing,' said the student, giving a light squeeze to the large, cold hand that was proffered him.

'I hope so,' replied the professor, stroking his gray cheek with his fingers. 'Yes, I hope so,' he repeated weightily, 'I hope so.'

The student gave the two suitcases standing next to the deck chair a cursory glance. One of them was a dignified veteran, covered with the white traces of old travel labels, like bird droppings on a monument. The other one – brand-new, orange-colored, with gleaming locks – for some reason caught his attention.

'Let me move that suitcase before it falls over,' he offered, to keep up the conversation.

The professor chuckled. He did look like that silver-browed comic, or else like an aging boxer . . .

'The suitcase, you say? Know what I have in it?' he inquired, with a hint of irritation in his voice. 'Can't guess? A marvelous object! A special kind of coat hanger . . .'

'A German invention, sir?' the student prompted, remembering that the biologist had just been to Berlin for a scientific congress.

The professor gave a hearty, creaking laugh, and a golden tooth flashed like a flame. 'A divine invention, my friend – divine. Something everybody needs. Why, you travel with the same kind of thing yourself. Eh? Or perhaps you're a polyp?' The student grinned. He knew

Revenge

that the professor was given to obscure jokes. The old man was the object of much gossip at the university. They said he tortured his spouse, a very young woman. The student had seen her once. A skinny thing, with incredible eyes. 'And how is your wife, sir?' asked the red-haired student.

The professor replied, 'I shall be frank with you, dear friend. I've been struggling with myself for quite sometime, but now I feel compelled to tell you . . . My dear friend, I like to travel in silence. I trust you'll forgive me.'

But here the student, whistling in embarrassment and sharing his sister's lot, departs forever from these pages.

The biology professor, meanwhile, pulled his black felt hat down over his bristly brows to shield his eyes against the sea's dazzling shimmer, and sank into a semblance of sleep. The sunlight falling on his gray, clean-shaven face, with its large nose and heavy chin, made it seem freshly modeled out of moist clay. Whenever a flimsy autumn cloud happened to screen the sun, the race would suddenly darken, dry out, and petrify. It was all, of course, alternating light and shade rather than a reflection of his thoughts. If his thoughts had indeed been reflected on his face, the professor would have hardly been a pretty sight. The trouble was that he had received a report the other day from the private detective he had hired in London that his wife was unfaithful to him. An intercepted letter, written in her minuscule, familiar hand, began, '*My dear darling Jack, I am still all full of your last kiss.*' The professor's name was certainly not Jack – that was the whole point. The perception made him feel neither surprise nor pain, not even masculine vexation, but only hatred, sharp and cold as a lancet. He realized with utter clarity that he would murder his wife. There could be no qualms. One had only to devise the most excruciating, the most ingenious method. As he reclined in the deck chair, he reviewed for the hundredth time all the methods of torture described by travelers and medieval scholars. Not one of them, so far, seemed adequately painful. In the distance, at the verge of the green shimmer, the sugary-white cliffs of Dover were materializing, and he had still not made a decision. The steamer fell silent and, gently rocking, docked. The professor followed his porter down the gangplank. The customs officer, after rattling off the items ineligible for import, asked him to open a suitcase – the new, orange one. The professor turned the lightweight key in its lock and swung open the leather flap. Some Russian lady behind him loudly exclaimed, 'Good Lord!' and gave a nervous laugh. Two Belgians standing on either side of the professor cocked their heads and gave a kind of upward glance. One shrugged his shoulders and the other gave a soft whistle, while the English turned away with indifference. The official, dumbfounded, goggled his eyes at the suitcase's contents. Everybody felt very creepy and uncomfortable. The biologist phlegmatically gave his name, mentioning the university museum. Expressions cleared up. Only a few ladies were chagrined to learn that no crime had been committed.

'But why do you transport it in a suitcase?' inquired the official with respectful reproach, gingerly lowering the flap and chalking a scrawl on the bright leather. 'I was in a hurry,' said the professor with a fatigued squint. 'No time to hammer together a crate. In any case it's a valuable object and not something I'd send in the baggage hold.' And, with a stooped but springy gait, the professor crossed to the railway platform past a policeman who resembled a gargantuan toy. But suddenly he paused as if remembering something and mumbled with a radiant, kindly smile, 'There – I have it. A most clever method.' Whereupon he heaved a sigh of relief and purchased two bananas, a pack of cigarettes, newspapers reminiscent of crackling bedsheets, and, a few minutes later, was speeding in a comfortable compartment of the Continental Express along the scintillating sea, the white cliffs, the emerald pastures of Kent.

2

They were wonderful eyes indeed, with pupils like glossy inkdrops on dove-gray satin. Her hair was cut short and golden-pale in hue, a luxuriant topping of fluff. She was small, upright, flat-chested. She had been expecting her husband since yesterday, and knew for certain he would arrive today. Wearing a gray, open-necked dress and velvet slippers, she was sitting on a peacock ottoman in the parlor, thinking what a pity it was her husband did not believe in ghosts and openly despised the young medium, a Scot with pale, delicate eyelashes, who occasionally visited her. After all, odd things did happen to her. Recently, in her sleep, she had had a vision of a dead youth with whom, before she was married, she had strolled in the twilight, when the blackberry blooms seem so ghostly white. Next morning, still aquiver, she had penciled a letter to him – a letter to her dream. In this letter she had lied to poor Jack. She had, in fact, nearly forgotten about him; she loved her excruciating husband with a fearful but faithful love; yet she wanted to send a little warmth to this dear spectral visitor, to reassure him with some words from earth. The letter vanished mysteriously from her writing pad, and the same night she dreamt of a long table, from under which Jack suddenly emerged, nodding to her gratefully. Now, for some reason, she felt uneasy when recalling that dream, almost as if she had cheated on her husband with a ghost.

The drawing room was warm and festive. On the wide, low windowsill lay a silk cushion, bright yellow with violet stripes.

The professor arrived just when she had decided his ship must have gone to the bottom. Glancing out the window, she saw the black top of a taxi, the driver's proffered palm, and the massive shoulders of her husband who had bent down his head as he paid. She flew through the rooms and trotted downstairs swinging her thin, bared arms.

He was climbing toward her, stooped, in an ample coat. Behind him a servant carried his suitcases.

She pressed against his woolen scarf, playfully bending back the heel of one slender, gray-stockinged leg. He kissed her warm temple. With a good-natured smile he lifted away her arms. 'I'm covered with dust . . . Wait . . .,' he mumbled, holding her by the wrists. Frowning, she tossed her head and the pale conflagration of her hair. The professor stooped and kissed her on the lips with another little grin.

At supper, thrusting out the white breastplate of his starched shirt and energetically moving his glossy cheekbones, he recounted his brief journey. He was reservedly jolly. The curved silk lapels of his dinner jacket his bulldog jaw, his massive bald head with ironlike veins on its temples – all this aroused in his wife an exquisite pity: the pity she always felt because, as he studied the minutiae of life, he refused to enter her world, where the poetry of de la Mare flowed and infinitely tender astral spirits hurtled.

'Well, did your ghosts come knocking while I was away?' he asked, reading her thoughts. She wanted to tell him about the dream, the letter, but felt somehow guilty.

'You know something,' he went on, sprinkling sugar on some pink rhubarb, 'you and your friends are playing with fire. There can be really terrifying occurrences. One Viennese doctor told me about some incredible metamorphoses the other day. Some woman – some kind of fortune-telling hysteric – died, of a heart attack I think, and, when the doctor undressed her (it all happened in a Hungarian hut, by candlelight), he was stunned at the sight of her body; it was entirely covered with a reddish sheen, was soft and slimy to the touch, and, upon closer examination, he realized that this plump, taut cadaver consisted entirely of narrow, circular bands of skin, as if it were all bound evenly and tightly by invisible strings, something like that advertisement for French tires, the man whose body is all tires. Except that in her case these tires were very thin and pale red. And, as the doctor watched, the corpse gradually began to unwind like a huge ball of yarn . . . Her body was a thin, endless worm, which was disentangling itself and crawling, slithering out through the crack under the door while, on the bed, there remained a naked, white, still humid skeleton. Yet this woman had a husband, who had once kissed her – kissed that worm.'

The professor poured himself a glass of port the color of mahogany and began gulping the rich liquid, without taking his narrowed eyes off his wife's face. Her thin, pale shoulders gave a shiver. 'You yourself don't realize what a terrifying thing you've told me,' she said in agitation. 'So the woman's ghost disappeared into a worm. It's all terrifying . . .'

'I sometimes think,' said the professor, ponderously shooting a cuff and examining his blunt fingers, 'that, in the final analysis, my science is an idle illusion, that it is we who have invented the laws of physics, that anything – absolutely anything – can happen. Those who abandon themselves to such thoughts go mad . . .'

He stifled a yawn, tapping his clenched fist against his lips.

'What's come over you, my dear?' his wife exclaimed softly. 'You never spoke this way before . . . I thought you knew everything, had everything mapped out . . .'

For an instant the professor's nostrils flared spasmodically, and a gold fang flashed. But his face quickly regained its flabby state. He stretched and got up from the table. 'I'm babbling nonsense,' he said calmly and tenderly. 'I'm tired. I'll go to bed. Don't turn on the light when you come in. Get right into bed with me – with me,' he repeated meaningfully and tenderly, as he had not spoken for a long time.

These words resounded gently within her when she remained alone in the drawing room.

She had been married to him for five years and, despite her husband's capricious disposition, his frequent outbursts of unjustified jealousy, his silences, sullenness, and incomprehension, she felt happy, for she loved and pitied him. She, all slender and white, and he, massive, bald, with tufts of gray wool in the middle of his chest, made an impossible, monstrous couple – and yet she enjoyed his infrequent, forceful caresses.

A chrysanthemum, in its vase on the mantel, dropped several curled petals with a dry rustle. She gave a start and her heart jolted disagreeably as she remembered that the air was always filled with phantoms, that even her scientist husband had noted their fearsome apparitions.

She recalled how Jackie had popped out from under the table and started nodding his head with an eerie tenderness. It seemed to her that all the objects in the room were watching her expectantly. She was chilled by a wind of fear. She quickly left the drawing room, restraining an absurd cry. She caught her breath and thought, What a silly thing I am, really . . . In the bathroom she spent a long time examining the sparkling pupils of her eyes. Her small face, capped by fluffy gold, seemed unfamiliar to her.

Feeling light as a young girl, with nothing on but a

lace nightgown, trying not to brush against the furniture, she went to the darkened bedroom. She extended her arms to locate the headboard of the bed, and lay down on its edge. She knew she was not alone, that her husband was lying beside her. For a few instants she motionlessly gazed upward, feeling the fierce, muffled pounding of her heart.

When her eyes had become accustomed to the dark, intersected by the stripes of moonlight pouring through the muslin blind, she turned her head toward her husband. He was lying with his back to her, wrapped in the blanket. All she could see was the bald crown of his head, which seemed extraordinarily sleek and white in the puddle of moonlight.

He's not asleep, she thought affectionately. If he were, he would be snoring a little.

She smiled and, with her whole body, slid over toward her husband, spreading her arms under the covers for the familiar embrace. Her fingers felt some smooth ribs. Her knee struck a smooth bone. A skull, its black eye sockets rotating, rolled from its pillow onto her shoulder.

Electric light flooded the room. The professor, in his crude dinner jacket, his starched bosom, eyes, and enormous forehead glistening, emerged from behind a screen and approached the bed.

The blanket and sheets, jumbled together, slithered to the rug. His wife lay dead, embracing the white, hastily cobbled skeleton of a hunchback that the professor had acquired abroad for the university museum.

A Forgotten Poet

I

In 1899, in the ponderous, comfortable padded St Petersburg of those days, a prominent cultural organization, the Society for the Advancement of Russian Literature, decided to honor in a grand way the memory of the poet Konstantin Perov, who had died half a century before at the ardent age of four-and-twenty. He had been styled the Russian Rimbaud and, although the French boy surpassed him in genius, such a comparison is not wholly unjustified. When only eighteen he composed his remarkable *Georgian Nights*, a long, rambling 'dream epic', certain passages of which rip the veil of its traditional Oriental setting to produce that heavenly draft which suddenly locates the sensorial effect of true poetry right between one's shoulder blades.

This was followed three years later by a volume of poems: he had got hold of some German philosopher or other, and several of these pieces are distressing because of the grotesque attempt at combining an authentic lyrical spasm with a metaphysical explanation of the universe; but the rest are still as vivid and unusual as they were in the days when that queer youth dislocated the

Russian vocabulary and twisted the necks of accepted epithets in order to make poetry splutter and scream instead of twittering. Most readers like best those poems of his where the ideas of emancipation, so characteristic of the Russian fifties, are expressed in a glorious storm of obscure eloquence, which, as one critic put it, 'does not show you the enemy but makes you fairly burst with the longing to fight.' Personally I prefer the purer and at the same time bumpier lyrics such as 'The Gypsy' or 'The Bat'.

Perov was the son of a small landowner of whom the only thing known is that he tried planting tea on his estate near Luga. Young Konstantin (to use a biographical intonation) spent most of his time in St Petersburg vaguely attending the university, then vaguely looking for a clerical job – little indeed is known of his activities beyond such trivialities as can be deduced from the general trends of his set. A passage in the correspondence of the famous poet Nekrasov, who happened to meet him once in a bookshop, conveys the image of a sulky, unbalanced, 'clumsy and fierce' young man with 'the eyes of a child and the shoulders of a furniture mover.'

He is also mentioned in a police report as 'conversing in low tones with two other students' in a coffeehouse on Nevsky Avenue. And his sister, who married a merchant from Riga, is said to have deplored the poet's emotional adventures with seamstresses and washerwomen. In the autumn of 1849 he visited his father with the special intent of obtaining money for a trip to Spain. His father, a man of simple reactions, slapped him on the face; and

A Forgotten Poet

a few days later the poor boy was drowned while bathing in the neighboring river. His clothes and a half-eaten apple were found lying under a birch tree, but the body was never recovered.

His fame was sluggish: a passage from the *Georgian Nights*, always the same one, in all anthologies; a violent article by the radical critic Dobrolyubov, in 1859, lauding the revolutionary innuendoes of his weakest poems; a general notion in the eighties that a reactionary atmosphere had thwarted and finally destroyed a fine if somewhat inarticulate talent – this was about all.

In the nineties, because of a healthier interest in poetry, coinciding as it sometimes does with a sturdy and dull political era, a flurry of rediscovery started around Perov's rhymes while, on the other hand, the liberal-minded were not averse to following Dobrolyubov's cue. The subscription for a monument in one of the public parks proved a perfect success. A leading publisher collected all the scraps of information available in regard to Perov's life and issued his complete works in one fairly plump volume. The monthlies contributed several scholarly surveys. The commemorative meeting in one of the best halls of the capital attracted a crowd.

2

A few minutes before the start, while the speakers were still assembled in a committee room behind the stage, the door opened gustily and there entered a sturdy old man, clad in a frock coat that had seen – on his or on somebody else's shoulders – better times. Without paying the slightest heed to the admonishments of a couple of ribbon-badged university students who, in their capacity of attendants, were attempting to restrain him, he proceeded with perfect dignity toward the committee, bowed, and said, 'I am Perov.'

A friend of mine, almost twice my age and now the only surviving witness of the event, tells me that the chairman (who as a newspaper editor had a great deal of experience in the matter of extravagant intruders) said without even looking up, 'Kick him out.' Nobody did – perhaps because one is apt to show a certain courtesy to an old gentleman who is supposedly very drunk. He sat down at the table and, selecting the mildest-looking person, Slavsky, a translator of Longfellow, Heine, and Sully-Prudhomme (and later a member of the terrorist group), asked in a matter-of-fact tone whether the 'monument money' had already been collected, and if so, when could he have it.

All the accounts agree on the singularly quiet way in which he made his claim. He did not press his point. He merely stated it as if absolutely unconscious of any possibility of his being disbelieved. What impressed one was that at the very beginning of that weird affair, in that secluded room, among those distinguished men, there he was with his patriarchal beard, faded brown eyes, and potato nose, sedately inquiring about the benefits from the proceedings without even bothering to produce such proofs as might have been faked by an ordinary impostor.

A Forgotten Poet

'Are you a relative?' asked someone.

'My name is Konstantin Konstantinovich Perov,' said the old man patiently. 'I am given to understand that a descendant of my family is in the hall, but that is neither here nor there.'

'How old are you?' asked Slavsky.

'I am seventy-four,' he replied, 'and the victim of several poor crops in succession.'

'You are surely aware,' remarked the actor Yermakov, 'that the poet whose memory we are celebrating tonight was drowned in the river Oredezh exactly fifty years ago.'

'*Vzdor*' ('Nonsense'), retorted the old man. 'I staged that business for reasons of my own.'

'And now, my dear fellow,' said the chairman, 'I really think you must go.'

They dismissed him from their consciousness and flocked out onto the severely lighted platform where another committee table, draped in solemn red cloth, with the necessary number of chairs behind it, had been hypnotizing the audience for some time with the glint of its traditional decanter. To the left of this, one could admire the oil painting loaned by the Sheremetevski Art Gallery: it represented Perov at twenty-two, a swarthy young man with romantic hair and an open shirt collar. The picture stand was piously camouflaged by means of leaves and flowers. A lectern with another decanter loomed in front and a grand piano was waiting in the wings to be rolled in later for the musical part of the program.

The hall was well packed with literary people, enlightened lawyers, schoolteachers, scholars, eager university students of both sexes, and the like. A few humble agents of the secret police had been delegated to attend the meeting in inconspicuous spots of the hall, as the government knew by experience that the most staid cultural assemblies had a queer knack of slipping into an orgy of revolutionary propaganda. The fact that one of Perov's first poems contained a veiled but benevolent allusion to the insurrection of 1825 suggested taking certain precautions: one never could tell what might happen after a public mouthing of such lines as 'the gloomy sough of Siberian larches communicates with the underground ore' ('*sibirskikh pikht oogrewmyi shorokh s podzemnoy snositsa roodoy*').

As one of the accounts has it, 'soon one became aware that something vaguely resembling a Dostoyevskian row [the author is thinking of a famous slapstick chapter in *The Possessed*] was creating an atmosphere of awkwardness and suspense.' This was due to the fact that the old gentleman deliberately followed the seven members of the jubilee committee onto the platform and then attempted to sit down with them at the table. The chairman, being mainly intent upon avoiding a scuffle in full view of the audience, did his best to make him desist. Under the public disguise of a polite smile he whispered to the patriarch that he would have him ejected from the hall if he did not let go the back of the chair which Slavsky, with a nonchalant air but with a grip of iron, was covertly

A Forgotten Poet

wresting from under the old man's gnarled hand. The old man refused but lost his hold and was left without a seat. He glanced around, noticed the piano stool in the wings, and coolly pulled it onto the stage just a fraction of a second before the hands of a screened attendant tried to snatch it back. He seated himself at some distance from the table and immediately became exhibit number one.

Here the committee made the fatal mistake of again dismissing his presence from their minds: they were, let it be repeated, particularly anxious to avoid a scene; and moreover, the blue hydrangea next to the picture stand half concealed the obnoxious party from their physical vision. Unfortunately, the old gentleman was most conspicuous to the audience, as he sat there on his unseemly pedestal (with its rotatory potentialities hinted at by a recurrent creaking), opening his spectacle case and breathing fishlike upon his glasses, perfectly calm and comfortable, his venerable head, shabby black clothes, and elastic-sided boots simultaneously suggesting the needy Russian professor and the prosperous Russian undertaker.

The chairman went up to the lectern and launched upon his introductory speech. Whisperings rippled all over the audience, for people were naturally curious to know who the old fellow was. Firmly bespectacled, with his hands on his knees, he peered sideways at the portrait, then turned away from it and inspected the front row. Answering glances could not help shuttling between the shiny dome of his head and the curly head of the portrait, for during the chairman's long speech the details of the intrusion spread, and the imagination of some started to toy with the idea that a poet belonging to an almost legendary period, snugly relegated to it by textbooks, an anachronistic creature, a live fossil in the nets of an ignorant fisherman, a kind of Rip Van Winkle, was actually attending in his drab dotage the reunion dedicated to the glory of his youth.

'. . . let the name of Perov,' said the chairman, ending his speech, 'be never forgotten by thinking Russia. Tyutchev has said that Pushkin will always be remembered by our country as a first love. In regard to Perov we may say that he was Russia's first experience in freedom. To a superficial observer this freedom may seem limited to Perov's phenomenal lavishness of poetical images which appeal more to the artist than to the citizen. But we, representatives of a more sober generation, are inclined to decipher for ourselves a deeper, more vital, more human, and more social sense in such lines of his as

> When the last snow hides in the shade of the cemetery wall
> and the coat of my neighbor's black horse
> shows a swift blue sheen in the swift April sun,
> and the puddles are as many heavens cupped in the Negro-hands of the Earth,
> then my heart goes out in its tattered cloak
> to visit the poor, the blind, the foolish,

> the round backs slaving for the round bellies,
> all those whose eyes dulled by care or lust do not see
> the holes in the snow, the blue horse, the miraculous puddle.

A burst of applause greeted this, but all of a sudden there was a break in the clapping, and then disharmonious gusts of laughter; for, as the chairman, still vibrating with the words he had just uttered, went back to the table, the bearded stranger got up and acknowledged the applause by means of jerky nods and awkward wavings of the hand, his expression combining formal gratitude with a certain impatience. Slavsky and a couple of attendants made a desperate attempt to bundle him away, but from the depth of the audience there arose the cries of 'Shame, shame!' and *'Astavte starika!'* ('Leave the old man alone!')

I find in one of the accounts the suggestion that there were accomplices among the audience, but I think that mass compassion, which may come as unexpectedly as mass vindictiveness, is sufficient to explain the turn things were taking. In spite of having to cope with three men the *'starik'* managed to retain a remarkable dignity of demeanor, and when his halfhearted assailants retired and he retrieved the piano stool that had been knocked down during the struggle, there was a murmur of satisfaction. However, the regrettable fact remained that the atmosphere of the meeting was hopelessly impaired. The younger and rowdier members of the audience were beginning to enjoy themselves hugely. The chairman, his nostrils quivering, poured himself out a tumbler of water. Two secret agents were cautiously exchanging glances from two different points of the house.

3

The speech of the chairman was followed by the treasurer's account of the sums received from various institutions and private persons for the erection of a Perov monument in one of the suburban parks. The old man unhurriedly produced a bit of paper and a stubby pencil and, propping the paper on his knee, began to check the figures which were being mentioned. Then the granddaughter of Perov's sister appeared for a moment on the stage. The organizers had had some trouble with this item of the program since the person in question, a fat, popeyed, waxpale young woman, was being treated for melancholia in a home for mental patients. With twisted mouth and all dressed up in pathetic pink, she was shown to the audience for a moment and then whisked back into the firm hands of a buxom woman delegated by the home.

When Yermakov, who in those days was the darling of theatergoers, a kind of *beau ténor* in terms of the drama, began delivering in his chocolate-cream voice the Prince's speech from the *Georgian Nights*, it became clear that even his best fans were more interested in the reactions of the old man than in the beauty of the delivery. At the lines

> If metal is immortal, then somewhere
> there lies the burnished button that I lost

upon my seventh birthday in a garden.
Find me that button and my soul will know
that every soul is saved and stored and treasured

a chink appeared for the first time in his composure and he slowly unfolded a large handkerchief and lustily blew his nose – a sound which sent Yermakov's heavily adumbrated, diamond-bright eye squinting like that of a timorous steed.

The handkerchief was returned to the folds of the coat and only several seconds *after* this did it become noticeable to the people in the first row that tears were trickling from under his glasses. He did not attempt to wipe them, though once or twice his hand did go up to his spectacles with claw-wise spread fingers, but it dropped again, as if by any such gesture (and this was the culminating point of the whole delicate masterpiece) he was afraid to attract attention to his tears. The tremendous applause that followed the recitation was certainly more a tribute to the old man's performance than to the poem in Yermakov's rendering. Then, as soon as the applause petered out, he stood up and marched toward the edge of the platform.

There was no attempt on the part of the committee to stop him, and this for two reasons. First, the chairman, driven to exasperation by the old man's conspicuous behavior, had gone out for a moment and given a certain order. In the second place, a medley of strange doubts was beginning to unnerve some of the organizers, so that there was a complete hush when the old man placed his elbows on the reading stand.

'And this is fame,' he said in such a husky voice that from the back rows there came cries of *'Gromche, gromche!'* ('Louder, louder!')

'I am saying that this is fame,' he repeated, grimly peering over his spectacles at the audience. 'A score of frivolous poems, words made to joggle and jingle, and a man's name is remembered as if he had been of some use to humanity! No, gentlemen, do not delude yourselves. Our empire and the throne of our father the Tsar still stand as they stood, akin to frozen thunder in their invulnerable might, and the misguided youth who scribbled rebellious verse half a century ago is now a law-abiding old man respected by honest citizens. An old man, let me add, who needs your protection. I am the victim of the elements: the land I had plowed with my sweat, the lambs I had personally suckled, the wheat I had seen waving its golden arms—'

It was then that two enormous policemen quickly and painlessly removed the old man. The audience had a glimpse of his being rushed out – his dickey protruding one way, his beard the other, a cuff dangling from his wrist, but still that gravity and that pride in his eyes.

When reporting the celebration, the leading dailies referred only in passing to the 'regrettable incident' that had marred it. But the disreputable *St. Petersburg Record*, a lurid and reactionary rag edited by the brothers Kherstov for the benefit of the lower middle class and of a blissfully semiliterate substratum of working people, blazed forth with a series of articles maintaining that the 'regrettable incident' was nothing less than the reappearance of the authentic Perov.

4

In the meantime, the old man had been collected by the very wealthy and vulgarly eccentric merchant Gromov, whose household was full of vagabond monks, quack doctors, and 'pogromystics.' The *Record* printed interviews with the impostor. In these the latter said dreadful things about the 'lackeys of the revolutionary party' who had cheated him of his identity and robbed him of his money. This money he proposed to obtain by law from the publishers of Perov's complete works. A drunken scholar attached to the Gromov household pointed out the (unfortunately rather striking) similarity between the old man's features and those of the portrait.

There appeared a detailed but most implausible account of his having staged a suicide in order to lead a Christian life in the bosom of Saint Russia. He had been everything: a peddler, a bird catcher, a ferryman on the Volga, and had wound up by acquiring a bit of land in a remote province. I have seen a copy of a sordid-looking booklet, *The Death and Resurrection of Konstantin Perov*, which used to be sold on the streets by shivering beggars, together with the *Adventures of the Marquis de Sade* and the *Memoirs of an Amazon*.

My best find, however, in looking through old files, is a smudgy photograph of the bearded impostor perched upon the marble of the unfinished Perov monument in a leafless park. He is seen standing very straight with his arms folded; he wears a round fur cap and a new pair of galoshes but no overcoat; a little crowd of his backers is gathered at his feet, and their little white faces stare into the camera with that special navel-eyed, self-complacent expression peculiar to old pictures of lynching parties.

Given this atmosphere of florid hooliganism and reactionary smugness (so closely linked up with governmental ideas in Russia, no matter whether the Tsar be called Alexander, Nicholas, or Joe), the intelligentsia could hardly bear to visualize the disaster of identifying the pure, ardent, revolutionary-minded Perov as represented by his poems with a vulgar old man wallowing in a painted pigsty. The tragic part was that while neither Gromov nor the Kherstov brothers really believed the purveyor of their fun was the true Perov, many honest, cultivated people had become obsessed by the impossible thought that what they had ejected was Truth and Justice.

As a recently published letter from Slavsky to Korolenko has it: 'One shudders to think that a gift of destiny unparalleled in history, the Lazarus-like resurrection of a great poet of the past, may be ungratefully ignored – nay, even more, deemed a fiendish deceit on the part of a man whose only crime has been half a century of silence and a few minutes of wild talk.' The wording is muddled but the gist is clear: intellectual Russia was less afraid of falling victim to a hoax than of sponsoring a hideous blunder. But there was something she was still more afraid of, and that was the destruction of an ideal; for your radical is ready to upset everything in the world except any such trivial bauble, no matter how doubtful and dusty, that for some reason radicalism has enshrined.

It is rumored that at a certain secret session of the Society for the Advancement of Russian Literature the numerous insulting epistles that the old man kept sending in were carefully compared by experts with a very old letter written by the poet in his teens. It had been discovered in a certain private archive, was believed to be the only sample of Perov's hand, and none except the scholars who pored over its faded ink knew of its existence. Neither do we know what their findings were.

It is further rumored that a lump of money was amassed and that the old man was approached without the knowledge of his disgraceful companions. Apparently, a substantial monthly pension was to be granted him under the condition that he return at once to his farm and stay there in decorous silence and oblivion. Apparently, too, the offer was accepted, for he vanished as jerkily as he had appeared, while Gromov consoled himself for the loss of his pet by adopting a shady hypnotizer of French extraction who a year or two later was to enjoy some success at the Court.

The monument was duly unveiled and became a great favorite with the local pigeons. The sales of the collected works fizzled out genteelly in the middle of a fourth edition. Finally, a few years later, in the region where Perov had been born, the oldest though not necessarily the brightest inhabitant told a lady journalist that he remembered his father telling him of finding a skeleton in a reedy part of the river.

5

This would have been all had not the Revolution come, turning up slabs of rich earth together with the white rootlets of little plants and fat mauve worms which otherwise would have remained buried. When, in the early twenties, in the dark, hungry, but morbidly active city, various odd cultural institutions sprouted (such as bookshops where famous but destitute writers sold their own books, and so on), somebody or other earned a couple of months' living by arranging a little Perov museum, and this led to yet another resurrection.

The exhibits? All of them except one (the letter). A secondhand past in a shabby hall. The oval-shaped eyes and brown locks of the precious Sheremetevsky portrait (with a crack in the region of the open collar suggesting a tentative beheading); a battered volume of the *Georgian Nights* that was thought to have belonged to Nekrasov; an indifferent photograph of the village school built on the spot where the poet's father had owned a house and an orchard. An old glove that some visitor to the museum had forgotten. Several editions of Perov's works distributed in such a way as to occupy the greatest possible space.

And because all these poor relics still refused to form a happy family, several period articles had been added, such as the dressing gown that a famous radical critic had worn in his rococo study, and the chains he had worn in his wooden Siberian prison. But there again, since neither this nor the portraits of various writers of the time were bulky enough, a model of the first railway train to run in Russia (in the forties, between St Petersburg and Tsarskoye Selo) had been installed in the middle of that dismal room.

The old man, now well over ninety but still articulate in speech and reasonably erect in carriage, would show you around the place as if he were your host instead of being the janitor. One had the odd impression that presently he would lead you into the next (non-existing) room, where supper would be served. All that he really possessed, however, was a stove behind a screen and the bench on which he slept; but if you bought one of the books exhibited for sale at the entrance he would autograph it for you as a matter of course.

Then one morning he was found dead on his bench by the woman who brought him his food. Three quarrelsome families lived for a while in the museum, and soon nothing remained of its contents. And as if some great hand with a great rasping sound had torn out a great bunch of pages from a number of books, or as if some frivolous story writer had bottled an imp of fiction in the vessel of truth, or as if . . .

But no matter. Somehow or other, in the next twenty years or so, Russia lost all contact with Perov's poetry. Young Soviet citizens know as little about his works as they do about mine. No doubt a time will come when he will be republished and readmired; still, one cannot help feeling that, as things stand, people are missing a great deal. One wonders also what future historians will make of the old man and his extraordinary contention. But that, of course, is a matter of secondary importance.

The Seaport

The low-ceilinged barbershop smelled of stale roses. Horseflies hummed hotly, heavily. The sunlight blazed on the floor in puddles of molten honey, gave the lotion bottles tweaks of sparkle, transluced through the long curtain hanging in the entrance, a curtain of clay beads and little sections of bamboo strung alternately on close-hung cord, which would disintegrate in an iridescent clitter-clatter every time someone entered and shouldered it aside. Before him, in the murkish glass, Nikitin saw his own tanned face, the long sculptured strands of his shiny hair, the glitter of the scissors that chirred above his ear, and his eyes were attentive and severe, as always happens when you contemplate yourself in mirrors. He had arrived in this ancient port in the south of France the day before, from Constantinople, where life had grown unbearable for him. That morning he had been to the Russian Consulate and the employment office, had roamed about the town, which, down narrow alleyways, crept sea-ward, and now, exhausted, prostrated by the heat, he had dropped in to have a haircut and to refresh his head. The floor around his chair was already strewn with small bright mice – the cuttings of his hair. The barber filled his palm with lather. A delicious chill ran through the crown of his head as the barber's fingers firmly rubbed in the thick foam. Then an icy gush made his heart jump, and a fluffy towel went to work on his face and his wet hair.

Parting the undulating curtain of rain with his shoulder, Nikitin went out into a steep alley. Its right side was in the shade; on the left a narrow stream quivered along the curb in the torrid radiance; a black-haired, toothless girl with swarthy freckles was collecting the shimmering rivulet with her resonant pail; and the stream, the sun, the violet shade – everything was flowing and slithering downward to the sea: another step and, in the distance, between some walls, loomed its compact sapphire brilliance. Infrequent pedestrians walked on the shady side. Nikitin happened upon a climbing Negro in a Colonial uniform, with a face like a wet galosh. On the sidewalk stood a straw chair from whose seat a cat departed with a cushioned bound. A brassy Provençal voice started jabbering in some window. A green shutter banged. On a vendor's stand, amid purple mollusks that gave off a whiff of seaweed, lay lemons shot with granulated gold.

Reaching the sea, Nikitin paused to look excitedly at the dense blue that, in the distance, modulated into blinding silver, and at the play of light delicately dappling the white topside of a yacht. Then, unsteady from the heat, he went in search of the small Russian restaurant whose address he had noted on a wall of the consulate.

The restaurant, like the barbershop, was hot and none too clean. In back, on a wide counter, appetizers and fruit showed through billows of protective grayish muslin. Nikitin sat down and squared his shoulders; his shirt stuck to his back. At a nearby table sat two Russians, evidently sailors of a French vessel, and, a little farther off, a solitary old fellow in gold-rimmed glasses was making smacking and sucking noises as he lapped borscht from his spoon. The proprietress, wiping her puffy hands with a towel, gave the newcomer a maternal look. Two shaggy pups were rolling on the floor in a flurry of little paws. Nikitin whistled, and a shabby old bitch with green mucus at the corners of her gentle eyes came and put her muzzle in his lap.

One of the seamen addressed him in a composed and unhurried tone: 'Send her away. She'll get fleas all over you.'

Nikitin cosseted the dog's head a little and raised his radiant eyes.

'Oh, I'm not afraid of that . . . Constantinople . . . The barracks . . . You can imagine . . .'

'Just get here?' asked the seaman. Even voice. Mesh T-shirt. All cool and competent. Dark hair neatly trimmed in back. Clear forehead. Overall appearance decent and placid.

'Last night,' Nikitin replied.

The borscht and the fiery dark wine made him sweat even more. He was happy to relax and have a peaceful chat. Bright sunlight poured through the aperture of the door together with the tremulous sparkle of the alley rivulet; from his corner under the gas meter, the elderly Russian's spectacles scintillated.

'Looking for work?' asked the other sailor, who was

middle-aged, blue-eyed, had a pale walrus mustache, and was also clean-cut, well groomed, levigated by sun and salty wind.

Nikitin said with a smile, 'I certainly am . . . Today I went to the employment office . . . They have jobs planting telegraph poles, weaving hawsers – I'm just not sure . . .'

'Come work with us,' said the black-haired one. 'As a stoker or something. No nonsense there, you can take my word . . . Ah, there you are, Lyalya – our profound respects!'

A young girl entered, wearing a white hat, with a sweet, plain face. She made her way among the tables and smiled, first at the puppies, then at the seamen. Nikitin had asked them something but forgot his question as he watched the girl and the motion of her low hips, by which you can always recognize a Russian damsel. The owner gave her daughter a tender look, as if to say, 'You poor tired thing,' for she had probably spent all morning in an office, or else worked in a store. There was something touchingly homespun about her that made you think of violet soap and a summer flag stop in a birch forest. There was no France outside the door, of course. Those mincing movements . . . Sunny nonsense.

'No, it's not complicated at all,' the seaman was saying, 'here's how it works – you have an iron bucket and a coal pit. You start scraping. Lightly at first, so long as the coal goes sliding down into the bucket by itself, then you scrape harder. When you've filled the bucket you set it on a cart. You roll it over to the chief stoker.

The Seaport

A bang of his shovel and – one! – the firebox door's open, a heave of the same shovel and – two! – in goes the coal – you know, fanned out so it will come down evenly. Precision work. Keep your eye on the dial, and if that pressure drops . . .'

In a window that gave on the street appeared the head and shoulders of a man wearing a panama and a white suit.

'How are you, Lyalya dearest?'

He leaned his elbows on the windowsill.

'Of course it *is* hot in there, a real furnace – you wear nothing to work but pants and a mesh T-shirt. The T-shirt is black when you're finished. As I was saying, about the pressure – "fur" forms in the fire-box, an incrustation hard as stone, which you break up with a poker this long. Tough work. But afterwards, when you pop out on deck, the sunshine feels cool even if you're in the tropics. You shower, then down you go to your quarters, straight into your hammock – that's heaven, let me tell you . . .'

Meanwhile, at the window: 'And he insists he saw me in a car, you see?' (Lyalya in a high-pitched, excited voice).

Her interlocutor, the gentleman in white, stood leaning on the sill from the outside, and the square window framed his rounded shoulders, his soft, shaven face half-lit by the sun – a Russian who had been lucky.

'He goes on to tell me I was wearing a lilac dress, when I don't even own a lilac dress,' yelped Lyalya, 'and he persists: *"zhay voo zasyur."*'

The seaman who had been talking to Nikitin turned and asked, 'Couldn't you speak Russian?'

The man in the window said, 'I managed to get this music, Lyalya. Remember?'

That was the momentary aura, and it felt almost deliberate, as if someone were having fun inventing this girl, this conversation, this small Russian restaurant in a foreign port – an aura of dear workaday provincial Russia, and right away, by some miraculous, secret association of thoughts, the world appeared grander to Nikitin, he yearned to sail the oceans, to put into legendary bays, to eavesdrop everywhere on other people's souls.

'You asked what run we're on? Indochina,' spontaneously said the seaman.

Nikitin pensively tapped a cigarette out of its case; a gold eagle was etched on the wooden lid.

'Must be wonderful.'

'What do you think? Sure it is.'

'Well, tell me about it. Something about Shanghai, or Colombo.'

'Shanghai? I've seen it. Warm drizzle, red sand. Humid as a greenhouse. As for Ceylon, for instance, I didn't get ashore to visit it – it was my watch, you know.'

Shoulders hunched, the white-jacketed man was saying something to Lyalya through the window, softly and significantly. She listened, her head cocked, fondling the dog's curled-over ear with one hand. Extending its fire-pink tongue, panting joyously and rapidly, the dog looked through the sunny chink of the door, most likely debating whether or not it was worthwhile to go lie

The Seaport

some more on the hot threshold. And the dog seemed to be thinking in Russian.

Nikitin asked, 'Where should I apply?'

The seaman winked at his mate, as if to say, 'See, I brought him round.' Then he said, 'It's very simple. Tomorrow morning bright and early you go to the Old Port, and at Pier Two you'll find our *Jean-Bart*. Have a chat with the first mate. I think he'll hire you.'

Nikitin took a keen and candid look at the man's clear, intelligent forehead. 'What were you before, in Russia?' he asked.

The man shrugged and gave a wry smile.

'What was he? A fool,' Droopy Mustache answered for him in a bass voice.

Later they both got up. The younger man pulled out the wallet he carried inserted in the front of his pants behind his belt buckle, in the manner of French sailors. Something elicited a high-pitched laugh from Lyalya as she came up and gave them her hand (palm probably a little damp). The pups were tumbling about the floor. The man standing at the window turned away, whistling absently and tenderly. Nikitin paid and went out leisurely into the sunlight.

It was about five in the afternoon. The sea's blueness, glimpsed at the far ends of alleys, hurt his eyes. The circular screens of the outdoor toilets were ablaze.

He returned to his squalid hotel and, slowly stretching his intertwined hands behind his head, collapsed onto the bed in a state of blissful solar inebriation. He dreamt he was an officer again, walking along a

Crimean slope overgrown with milkweed and oak shrubs, mowing off the downy heads of thistles as he went. He awoke because he had started laughing in his sleep; he awoke, and the window had already turned a twilight blue.

He leaned out into the cool chasm, meditating: Wandering women. Some of them Russian. What a big star.

He smoothed his hair, rubbed the dust off the knobby tips of his shoes with a corner of the blanket, checked his wallet – only five francs left – and went out to roam some more and revel in his solitary idleness.

Now it was more crowded than it had been in the afternoon. Along the alleys that descended toward the sea, people were sitting, cooling off. Girl in a kerchief with spangles... Flutter of eyelashes... Paunchy shopkeeper, sitting astride a straw chair, elbows propped on its reversed back, smoking, with a flap of shirt protruding on his belly from beneath his unbuttoned waistcoat. Children hopping in a squatting posture as they sailed little paper boats, by the light of a streetlamp, in the black streamlet running next to the narrow sidewalk. There were smells of fish and wine. From the sailors' taverns, which shone with a yellow gleam, came the labored sound of hurdy-gurdies, the pounding of palms on tables, metallic exclamations. And, in the upperpart of town, along the main avenue, the evening crowds shuffled and laughed, and women's slender ankles and the white shoes of naval officers flashed beneath clouds of acacias. Here and there, like the colored flames of some petrified fireworks display, cafés blazed in the purple twilight. Round tables right out on the sidewalk, shadows of black plane trees on the striped awning, illuminated from within. Nikitin stopped, picturing a mug of beer, ice-cold and heavy. Inside, beyond the tables, a violin wrung its sounds as if they were human hands, accompanied by the full-bodied resonance of a rippling harp. The more banal the music, the closer it is to the heart.

At an outer table sat a weary streetwalker all in green, swinging the pointed tip of her shoe.

I'll have the beer, decided Nikitin. No I won't . . . Then again . . .

The woman had doll-like eyes. There was something very familiar about those eyes, about those elongated, shapely legs. Gathering up her purse, she got up as if in a hurry to get somewhere. She wore a long jacketlike top of knitted emerald silk that adhered low on her hips. Past she went, squinting from the music.

It would be strange indeed, mused Nikitin. Something akin to a falling star hurtled through his memory, and, forgetting about his beer, he followed her as she turned into a dark, glistening alley. A streetlamp stretched her shadow. The shadow flashed along a wall and skewed. She walked slowly and Nikitin checked his pace, afraid, for some reason, to overtake her.

Yes, there's no question . . . God, this is wonderful . . .

The woman stopped on the curb. A crimson bulb burned over a black door. Nikitin walked past, came back, circled the woman, stopped. With a cooing laugh she uttered a French word of endearment.

In the wan light, Nikitin saw her pretty, fatigued face, and the moist luster of her minute teeth.

'Listen,' he said in Russian, simply and softly. 'We've known each other a long time, so why not speak our native language?'

She raised her eyebrows. 'Inglish? Yew spik Inglish?'

Nikitin gave her an intent look, then repeated somewhat helplessly, 'Come, you know and I know.'

'*T'es Polonais, alors?*' inquired the woman, dragging out the final rolled syllable as they do in the South.

Nikitin gave up with a sardonic smile, thrust a five-franc note into her hand, turned quickly, and started across the sloping square. An instant later he heard rapid footfalls behind him, and breathing, and the rustle of a dress. He looked back. There was no one. The square was deserted and dark. The night wind propelled a newspaper sheet across the flagstones.

He heaved a sigh, smiled once more, thrust his fists deep into his pockets, and, looking at the stars, which flashed and waned as if fanned by a gigantic bellows, began descending seaward. He sat down on the ancient wharf with his feet dangling over the edge, above the rhythmic, moonlit swaying of the waves, and sat thus for a long time, head thrown back, leaning on the palms of his stretched-back hands.

A falling star shot by with the suddenness of a missed heartbeat. A strong, clean gust blew through his hair, pale in the nocturnal radiance.

Razor

His regimental comrades had good reason to dub him 'Razor'. The man's face lacked a façade. When his acquaintances thought of him they could imagine him only in profile, and that profile was remarkable: nose sharp as a draftsman's triangle; chin sturdy as an elbow; long, soft eyelashes characteristic of certain very obstinate, very cruel people. His name was Ivanov.

That nickname of former days contained a strange clairvoyance. It is not rare for a man called Stone or Stein to become a perfectly good mineralogist. Captain Ivanov, after an epic escape and sundry insipid ordeals, had ended up in Berlin, and chosen the very trade at which his nickname had hinted – that of a barber.

He worked in a small but clean barbershop that also employed two young professionals, who treated 'the Russian captain' with jovial respect. Then there was the owner, a dour lump of a man who would spin the handle of the cash register with a silvery sound, and also a manicurist, anemic and translucent as if she had been drained dry by the contact of innumerable fingers placed, in batches of five, on the small velvet cushion in front of her.

Ivanov was very good at his work, although he was

somewhat handicapped by his poor knowledge of German. However, he soon figured out how to deal with the problem: tack a *'nicht'* onto the first sentence, an interrogative *'was?'* onto the next, then *'nicht'* again, continuing to alternate in the same way. And even though it was only in Berlin that he had learned haircutting, it was remarkable how closely his manner resembled that of the tonsors back in Russia, with their well-known penchant for a lot of superfluous scissor-clicking – they'll click away, take aim, and snip a lock or two, then keep their blades going lickety-split in the air as if impelled by inertia. This deft, gratuitous whirring was the very thing that earned him the respect of his colleagues.

Without doubt scissors and razors are weapons, and there was something about this metallic chirr that gratified Ivanov's warlike soul. He was a rancorous, keen-witted man. His vast, noble, splendid homeland had been ruined by some dull buffoon for the sake of a well-turned scarlet phrase, and this he could not forgive. Like a tightly coiled spring, vengeance lurked, biding its time, within his soul.

One very hot, bluish summer morning, taking advantage of the nearly total absence of customers during those workaday hours, both of Ivanov's colleagues took an hour off. Their employer, dying from the heat and from long-ripening desire, had silently escorted the pale, unresisting little manicurist to a back room. Left alone in the sun-drenched shop, Ivanov glanced through one newspaper, then lit a cigarette and, all in white, stepped outside the doorway and started watching the passersby.

Razor

People flashed past, accompanied by their blue shadows, which broke over the edge of the sidewalk and glided fearlessly underneath the glittering wheels of cars that left ribbonlike imprints on the heat-softened asphalt, resembling the ornate lacework of snakes. Suddenly a short, thickset gentleman in black suit and bowler, with a black briefcase under his arm, turned off the sidewalk and headed straight for white Ivanov. Blinking from the sun, Ivanov stepped aside to let him into the barbershop.

The newcomer's reflection appeared in all the mirrors at once: in profile, three-quarter-face, and showing the waxen bald spot in back from which the black bowler had ascended to snag a hat hook. And when the man turned squarely toward the mirrors, which sparkled above marble surfaces aglitter with green and gold scent bottles, Ivanov instantly recognized that mobile, puffy face with the piercing little eyes and a plump mole by the right lobe of his nose.

The gentleman silently sat down in front of the mirror, then, mumbling indistinctly, tapped his untidy cheek with a stubby finger: Meaning, I want a shave. In a kind of astonished haze, Ivanov spread a sheet over him, whipped up some tepid lather in a porcelain bowl, started brushing it on to the man's cheeks, rounded chin, and upper lip, gingerly circumnavigated the mole, began rubbing in the foam with his index finger. But he did all this mechanically, so shaken was he by having encountered this person again.

Now a flimsy white mask of soap covered the man's face up to his eyes, minuscule eyes that glittered like the tiny wheels of a watch movement. Ivanov had opened his razor and begun to sharpen it on a strap when he recovered from his amazement and realized that this man was in his power.

Then, bending over the waxy bald spot, he brought the blue blade close to the soapy mask and said very softly, 'My respects to you, comrade. How long has it been since you left our part of the world? No, don't move, please, or I might cut you prematurely.'

The glittering little wheels started moving faster, glanced at Ivanov's sharp profile, and stopped. Ivanov removed some excess flakes of lather with the blunt side of the razor and continued, 'I remember you very well, comrade. Sorry if I find it distasteful to pronounce your name. I remember how you interrogated me some six years ago, in Kharkov. I remember your signature, dear friend . . . But, as you see, I am still alive.'

Then the following happened. The little eyes darted about, then suddenly shut tight, eyelids compressed like those of the savage who thought closing his eyes made him invisible.

Ivanov tenderly moved his blade along the cold, rustling cheek.

'We're absolutely alone, comrade. Understand? One little slip of the razor, and right away there will be a good deal of blood. Here is where the carotid throbs. So there will be a good deal, even a great deal of blood. But first I want your face decently shaved, and, besides, I have something to recount to you.'

Cautiously, with two fingers, Ivanov lifted the fleshy

tip of the man's nose and, with the same tenderness, began shaving above the upper lip.

'The point, comrade, is that I remember everything. I remember perfectly, and I want you to remember too . . .' And, in a soft voice, Ivanov began his account, as he unhurriedly shaved the recumbent, motionless face. The tale he told must have been terrifying indeed, because from time to time his hand would stop, and he would stoop very close to the gentleman sitting like a corpse under the shroudlike sheet, his convex eyelids lowered.

'That is all,' Ivanov said with a sigh, 'that's the whole story. Tell me, what do you think would be a suitable atonement for all that? What is considered an equivalent of a sharp sword? And again, keep in mind that we are utterly, totally alone.

'Corpses are always shaved,' went on Ivanov, running the blade upward along the stretched skin of the man's neck. 'Those sentenced to death are shaved too. And now I am shaving you. Do you realize what is going to happen next?'

The man sat without stirring or opening his eyes. Now the lathery mask was gone from his face. Traces of foam remained only on his cheekbones and near his ears. This tensed, eyeless, fat face was so pallid that Ivanov wondered if he had not suffered a fit of paralysis. But when he pressed the flat surface of the razor to the man's neck, his entire body gave a twitch. He did not, however, open his eyes.

Ivanov gave the man's face a quick wipe and spat

some talcum on him from a pneumatic dispenser. 'That will do for you,' he said. 'I'm satisfied. You may leave.' With squeamish haste he yanked the sheet off the man's shoulders. The other remained seated.

'Get up, you ninny,' shouted Ivanov, pulling him up by the sleeve. The man froze, with firmly shut eyes, in the middle of the shop. Ivanov clapped the bowler on his head, thrust the briefcase under his arm, and swiveled him toward the door. Only then did the man jerk into motion. His shut-eyed face flashed in all the mirrors. He stepped like an automaton through the door that Ivanov was holding open, and, with the same mechanical gait, clutching his briefcase with an outstretched petrified hand, gazing into the sunny blur of the street with the glazed eyes of a Greek statue, he was gone.

First Love

1

In the early years of this century, a travel agency on Nevski Avenue displayed a three-foot-long model of an oak-brown international sleeping car. In delicate verisimilitude it completely outranked the painted tin of my clockwork trains. Unfortunately it was not for sale. One could make out the blue upholstery inside, the embossed leather lining of the compartment walls, their polished panels, inset mirrors, tulip-shaped reading lamps, and other maddening details. Spacious windows alternated with narrower ones, single or geminate, and some of these were of frosted glass. In a few of the compartments, the beds had been made.

The then great and glamorous Nord Express (it was never the same after World War I), consisting solely of such international cars and running but twice a week, connected St Petersburg with Paris. I would have said: directly with Paris, had passengers not been obliged to change from one train to a superficially similar one at the Russo-German frontier (Verzhbolovo-Eydtkuhnen), where the ample and lazy Russian sixty-and-a-half-inch gauge was replaced by the fifty-six-and-a-half-inch standard of Europe and coal succeeded birch logs.

In the far end of my mind I can unravel, I think, at least five such journeys to Paris, with the Riviera or Biarritz as their ultimate destination. In 1909, the year I now single out, my two small sisters had been left at home with nurses and aunts. Wearing gloves and a traveling cap, my father sat reading a book in the compartment he shared with our tutor. My brother and I were separated from them by a washroom. My mother and her maid occupied a compartment adjacent to ours. The odd one of our party, my father's valet, Osip (whom, a decade later, the pedantic Bolsheviks were to shoot, because he appropriated our bicycles instead of turning them over to the nation), had a stranger for companion.

In April of that year, Peary had reached the North Pole. In May, Chaliapin had sung in Paris. In June, bothered by rumors of new and better zeppelins, the United States War Department had told reporters of plans for an aerial navy. In July, Blériot had flown from Calais to Dover (with a little additional loop when he lost his bearings). It was late August now. The firs and marshes of northwestern Russia sped by, and on the following day gave way to German pine barrens and heather.

At a collapsible table, my mother and I played a card game called *durachki*. Although it was still broad daylight, our cards, a glass, and on a different plane the locks of a suitcase were reflected in the window. Through forest and field, and in sudden ravines, and among scuttling cottages, those discarnate gamblers kept steadily playing on for steadily sparkling stakes.

'*Ne budet-li, tï ved' ustali?*' ('Haven't you had enough, aren't you tired?') my mother would ask, and then would be lost in thought as she slowly shuffled the cards. The door of the compartment was open and I could see the corridor window, where the wires – six thin black wires – were doing their best to slant up, to ascend skyward, despite the lightning blows dealt them by one telegraph pole after another; but just as all six, in a triumphant swoop of pathetic elation, were about to reach the top of the window, a particularly vicious blow would bring them down, as low as they had ever been, and they would have to start all over again.

When, on such journeys as these, the train changed its pace to a dignified amble and all but grazed housefronts and shop signs, as we passed through some big German town, I used to feel a twofold excitement, which terminal stations could not provide. I saw a city with its toylike trams, linden trees, and brick walls enter the compartment, hobnob with the mirrors, and fill to the brim the windows on the corridor side. This informal contact between train and city was one part of the thrill. The other was putting myself in the place of some passerby who, I imagined, was moved as I would be moved myself to see the long, romantic, auburn cars, with their intervestibular connecting curtains as black as bat wings and their metal lettering copper-bright in the low sun, unhurriedly negotiate an iron bridge across an everyday thoroughfare and then turn, with all windows suddenly ablaze, around a last block of houses.

There were drawbacks to those optical amalgamations. The wide-windowed dining car, a vista of chaste bottles of mineral water, miter-folded napkins, and dummy chocolate bars (whose wrappers – Cailler, Kohler, and so forth – enclosed nothing but wood) would be perceived at first as a cool haven beyond a consecution of reeling blue corridors; but as the meal progressed toward its fatal last course, one would keep catching the car in the act of being recklessly sheathed, lurching waiters and all, in the landscape, while the landscape itself went through a complex system of motion, the daytime moon stubbornly keeping abreast of one's plate, the distant meadows opening fanwise, the near trees sweeping up on invisible swings toward the track, a parallel rail line all at once committing suicide by anastomosis, a bank of nictitating grass rising, rising, rising, until the little witness of mixed velocities was made to disgorge his portion of *omelette aux confitures de fraises*.

It was at night, however, that the *Compagnie Internationale des Wagons-Lits et des Grands Express Européens* lived up to the magic of its name. From my bed under my brother's bunk (Was he asleep? Was he there at all?), in the semidarkness of our compartment, I watched things, and parts of things, and shadows, and sections of shadows cautiously moving about and getting nowhere. The woodwork gently creaked and crackled. Near the door that led to the toilet, a dim garment on a peg and, higher up, the tassel of the blue, bivalved night-light swung rhythmically. It was hard to correlate those halting approaches, that hooded stealth, with the headlong rush of the outside night, which I knew *was* rushing by, spark-streaked, illegible.

I would put myself to sleep by the simple act of identifying myself with the engine driver. A sense of drowsy well-being invaded my veins as soon as I had everything nicely arranged – the carefree passengers in their rooms enjoying the ride I was giving them, smoking, exchanging knowing smiles, nodding, dozing; the waiters and cooks and train guards (whom I had to place somewhere) carousing in the diner; and myself, goggled and begrimed, peering out of the engine cab at the tapering track, at the ruby or emerald point in the black distance. And then, in my sleep, I would see something totally different – a glass marble rolling under a grand piano or a toy engine lying on its side with its wheels still working gamely.

A change in the speed of the train sometimes interrupted the current of my sleep. Slow lights were stalking by; each, in passing; investigated the same chink, and then a luminous compass measured the shadows. Presently, the train stopped with a long-drawn Westinghousian sigh. Something (my brother's spectacles, as it proved next day) fell from above. It was marvelously exciting to move to the foot of one's bed, with part of the bedclothes following, in order to undo cautiously the catch of the window shade, which could be made to slide only halfway up, impeded as it was by the edge of the upper berth.

Like moons around Jupiter, pale moths revolved about a lone lamp. A dismembered newspaper stirred on a bench. Somewhere on the train one could hear muffled voices, somebody's comfortable cough. There was nothing particularly interesting in the portion of station platform before me, and still I could not tear myself away from it until it departed of its own accord.

Next morning, wet fields with misshapen willows along the radius of a ditch or a row of poplars afar, traversed by a horizontal band of milky-white mist, told one that the train was spinning through Belgium. It reached Paris at four p.m.; and even if the stay was only an overnight one, I had always time to purchase something – say, a little brass *Tour Eiffel*, rather roughly coated with silver paint – before we boarded at noon on the following day the Sud Express, which, on its way to Madrid, dropped us around ten p.m. at the La Négresse station of Biarritz, a few miles from the Spanish frontier.

2

Biarritz still retained its quiddity in those days. Dusty blackberry bushes and weedy *terrains à vendre* bordered the road that led to our villa. The Carlton was still being built. Some thirty-six years had to elapse before Brigadier General Samuel McCroskey would occupy the royal suite of the Hotel du Palais, which stands on the site of a former palace, where, in the sixties, that incredibly agile medium, Daniel Home, is said to have been caught stroking with his bare foot (in imitation of a ghost hand)

First Love

the kind, trustful face of Empress Eugénie. On the promenade near the Casino, an elderly flower girl, with carbon eyebrows and a painted smile, nimbly slipped the plump torus of a carnation into the buttonhole of an intercepted stroller whose left jowl accentuated its royal fold as he glanced down sideways at the coy insertion of the flower.

Along the back line of the *plage*, various seaside chairs and stools supported the parents of straw-hatted children who were playing in front on the sand. I could be seen on my knees trying to set a found comb aflame by means of a magnifying glass. Men sported white trousers that to the eye of today would look as if they had comically shrunk in the washing; ladies wore, that particular season, light coats with silk-faced lapels, hats with big crowns and wide brims, dense embroidered white veils, frill-fronted blouses, frills at their wrists, frills on their parasols. The breeze salted one's lips. At a tremendous pace a stray golden-orange butterfly came dashing across the palpitating *plage*.

Additional movement and sound were provided by vendors hawking *cacahuètes*, sugared violets, pistachio ice cream of a heavenly green, cachou pellets, and huge convex pieces of dry, gritty, waferlike stuff that came from a red barrel. With a distinctness that no later superpositions have dimmed, I see that waffleman stomp along through deep mealy sand, with the heavy cask on his bent back. When called, he would sling it off his shoulder by a twist of its strap, bang it down on the sand in a Tower of Pisa position, wipe his face with his sleeve, and proceed to manipulate a kind of arrow-and-dial arrangement with numbers on the lid of the cask. The arrow rasped and whirred around. Luck was supposed to fix the size of a sou's worth of wafer. The bigger the piece, the more I was sorry for him.

The process of bathing took place on another part of the beach. Professional bathers, burly Basques in black bathing suits, were there to help ladies and children enjoy the terrors of the surf. Such a *baigneur* would place you with your back to the incoming wave and hold you by the hand as the rising, rotating mass of foamy, green water violently descended upon you from behind, knocking you off your feet with one mighty wallop. After a dozen of these tumbles, the *baigneur*, glistening like a seal, would lead his panting, shivering, moistly snuffling charge landward, to the flat foreshore, where an unforgettable old woman with gray hairs on her chin promptly chose a bathing robe from several hanging on a clothesline. In the security of a little cabin, one would be helped by yet another attendant to peel off one's soggy, sand-heavy bathing suit. It would plop onto the boards, and, still shivering, one would step out of it and trample on its bluish, diffuse stripes. The cabin smelled of pine. The attendant, a hunchback with beaming wrinkles, brought a basin of steaming-hot water, in which one immersed one's feet. From him I learned, and have preserved ever since in a glass cell of my memory, that 'butterfly' in the Basque language is *misericoletea* – or at least it sounded so (among the seven words I have found in dictionaries the closest approach is *micheletea*).

3

On the browner and wetter part of the *plage*, that part which at low tide yielded the best mud for castles, I found myself digging, one day, side by side with a little French girl called Colette.

She would be ten in November, I had been ten in April. Attention was drawn to a jagged bit of violet mussel shell upon which she had stepped with the bare sole of her narrow long-toed foot. No, I was not English. Her greenish eyes seemed flecked with the overflow of the freckles that covered her sharp-featured face. She wore what might now be termed a playsuit, consisting of a blue jersey with rolled-up sleeves and blue knitted shorts. I had taken her at first for a boy and then had been puzzled by the bracelet on her thin wrist and the corkscrew brown curls dangling from under her sailor cap.

She spoke in birdlike bursts of rapid twitter, mixing governess English and Parisian French. Two years before, on the same *plage*, I had been much attached to the lovely, suntanned little daughter of a Serbian physician; but when I met Colette, I knew at once that this was the real thing. Colette seemed to me so much stranger than all my other chance playmates at Biarritz! I somehow acquired the feeling that she was less happy than I, less loved. A bruise on her delicate, downy forearm gave rise to awful conjectures. 'He pinches as bad as my mummy,' she said, speaking of a crab. I evolved various schemes to save her from her parents, who were *'des bourgeois de Paris'* as I heard somebody tell my mother with a slight shrug. I interpreted the disdain in my own fashion, as I knew that those people had come all the way from Paris in their blue-and-yellow limousine (a fashionable adventure in those days) but had drably sent Colette with her dog and governess by an ordinary coach train. The dog was a female fox terrier with bells on her collar and a most waggly behind. From sheer exuberance, she would lap up salt water out of Colette's toy pail. I remember the sail, the sunset, and the lighthouse pictured on that pail, but I cannot recall the dog's name, and this bothers me.

During the two months of our stay at Biarritz, my passion for Colette all but surpassed my passion for butterflies. Since my parents were not keen to meet hers, I saw her only on the beach; but I thought of her constantly. If I noticed she had been crying, I felt a surge of helpless anguish that brought tears to my own eyes. I could not destroy the mosquitoes that had left their bites on her frail neck, but I could, and did, have a successful fistfight with a red-haired boy who had been rude to her. She used to give me warm handfuls of hard candy. One day, as we were bending together over a starfish, and Colette's ringlets were tickling my ear, she suddenly turned toward me and kissed me on the cheek. So great was my emotion that all I could think of saying was, 'You little monkey.'

I had a gold coin that I assumed would pay for our elopement. Where did I want to take her? Spain? America? The mountains above Pau? *'Là-bas, là-bas, dans la montagne,'* as I had heard Carmen sing at the opera. One strange night, I lay awake, listening to the recurrent thud of the ocean and

First Love

planning our flight. The ocean seemed to rise and grope in the darkness and then heavily fall on its face.

Of our actual getaway, I have little to report. My memory retains a glimpse of her obediently putting on rope-soled canvas shoes, on the lee side of a flapping tent, while I stuffed a folding butterfly net into a brown paper bag. The next glimpse is of our evading pursuit by entering a pitch-dark cinema near the Casino (which, of course, was absolutely out of bounds). There we sat, holding hands across the dog, which now and then gently jingled in Colette's lap, and were shown a jerky, drizzly, but highly exciting bullfight at San Sebastián. My final glimpse is of myself being led along the promenade by my tutor. His long legs move with a kind of ominous briskness and I can see the muscles of his grimly set jaw working under the tight skin. My bespectacled brother, aged nine, whom he happens to hold with his other hand, keeps trotting out forward to peer at me with awed curiosity, like a little owl.

Among the trivial souvenirs acquired at Biarritz before leaving, my favorite was not the small bull of black stone and not the sonorous sea-shell but something which now seems almost symbolic – a meerschaum penholder with a tiny peephole of crystal in its ornamental part. One held it quite close to one's eye, screwing up the other, and when one had got rid of the shimmer of one's own lashes, a miraculous photographic view of the bay and of the line of cliffs ending in a lighthouse could be seen inside.

And now a delightful thing happens. The process of re-creating that penholder and the microcosm in its eyelet stimulates my memory to a last effort. I try again to recall the name of Colette's dog – and, sure enough, along those remote beaches, over the glossy evening sands of the past, where each footprint slowly fills up with sunset water, here it comes, here it comes, echoing and vibrating: Floss, Floss, Floss!

Colette was back in Paris by the time we stopped there for a day before continuing our homeward journey; and there, in a fawn park under a cold blue sky, I saw her (by arrangement between our mentors, I believe) for the last time. She carried a hoop and a short stick to drive it with, and everything about her was extremely proper and stylish in an autumnal, Parisian, *tenue-de-ville-pour-fillettes* way. She took from her governess and slipped into my brother's hand a farewell present, a box of sugar-coated almonds, meant, I knew, solely for me; and instantly she was off, tap-tapping her glinting hoop through light and shade, around and around a fountain choked with dead leaves near which I stood. The leaves mingle in my memory with the leather of her shoes and gloves, and there was, I remember, some detail in her attire (perhaps a ribbon on her Scottish cap, or the pattern of her stockings) that reminded me then of the rainbow spiral in a glass marble. I still seem to be holding that wisp of iridescence, not knowing exactly where to fit it, while she runs with her hoop ever faster around me and finally dissolves among the slender shadows cast on the graveled path by the interlaced arches of its low looped fence.

The Wood-Sprite

I was pensively penning the outline of the inkstand's circular, quivering shadow. In a distant room a clock struck the hour, while I, dreamer that I am, imagined someone was knocking at the door, softly at first, then louder and louder. He knocked twelve times and paused expectantly.

'Yes, I'm here, come in . . .'

The doorknob creaked timidly, the flame of the runny candle tilted, and he hopped sidewise out of a rectangle of shadow, hunched, gray, powdered with the pollen of the frosty, starry night.

I knew his face – oh, how long I had known it!

His right eye was still in the shadows, the left peered at me timorously, elongated, smoky-green. The pupil glowed like a point of rust . . . That mossy-gray tuft on his temple, the pale-silver, scarcely noticeable eyebrow, the comical wrinkle near his whiskerless mouth – how all this teased and vaguely vexed my memory!

I got up. He stepped forward.

His shabby little coat seemed to be buttoned wrong – on the female side. In his hand he held a cap – no, a dark-colored, poorly tied bundle, and there was no sign of any cap . . .

Yes, of course I knew him – perhaps had even been fond of him, only I simply could not place the where and the when of our meetings. And we must have met often, otherwise I would not have had such a firm recollection of those cranberry lips, those pointy ears, that amusing Adam's apple . . .

With a welcoming murmur I shook his light, cold hand, and touched the back of a shabby armchair. He perched like a crow on a tree stump, and began speaking hurriedly.

'It's so scary in the streets. So I dropped in. Dropped in to visit you. Do you recognize me? You and I, we used to romp together and halloo at each other for days at a time. Back in the old country. Don't tell me you've forgotten?'

His voice literally blinded me. I felt dazzled and dizzy – I remembered the happiness, the echoing, endless, irreplaceable happiness . . .

No, it can't be: I'm alone . . . It's only some capricious delirium. Yet there really was somebody sitting next to me, bony and implausible, with long-eared German bootees, and his voice tintinnabulated, rustled – golden, luscious-green, familiar – while the words were so simple, so human . . .

'There – you remember. Yes, I am a former Forest Elf, a mischievous sprite. And here I am, forced to flee like everyone else.'

He heaved a deep sigh, and once again I had visions of billowing nimbus, lofty leafy undulations, bright flashes of birch bark like splashes of sea foam, against a dulcet,

The Wood-Sprite

perpetual, hum . . . He bent toward me and glanced gently into my eyes. 'Remember our forest, fir so black, birch all white? They've cut it all down. The grief was unbearable – I saw my dear birches crackling and falling, and how could I help? Into the marshes they drove me, I wept and I howled, I boomed like a bittern, then left lickety-split for a neighboring pine-wood.

'There I pined, and could not stop sobbing. I had barely grown used to it, and lo, there was no more pinewood, just blue-tinted cinders. Had to do some more tramping. Found myself a wood – a wonderful wood it was, thick, dark, and cool. Yet somehow it was just not the same thing. In the old days I'd frolic from dawn until dusk, whistle furiously, clap my hands, frighten passersby. You remember yourself – you lost your way once in a dark nook of my woods, you and some little white dress, and I kept tying the paths up in knots, spinning the tree trunks, twinkling through the foliage. Spent the whole night playing tricks. But I was only fooling around, it was all in jest, vilify me as they might. But now I sobered up, for my new abode was not a merry one. Day and night strange things crackled around me. At first I thought a fellow elf was lurking there; I called, then listened. Something crackled, something rumbled . . . But no, those were not the kinds of sounds we make. Once, toward evening, I skipped out into a glade, and what do I see? People lying around, some on their backs, some on their bellies. Well, I think, I'll wake them up, I'll get them moving! And I went to work shaking boughs, bombarding with cones, rustling, hooting . . . I toiled away for a whole hour, all to no avail. Then I took a closer look, and I was horror-struck. Here's a man with his head hanging by one flimsy crimson thread, there's one with a heap of thick worms for a stomach . . . I could not endure it. I let out a howl, jumped in the air, and off I ran . . .

'Long I wandered through different forests, but I could find no peace. Either it was stillness, desolation, mortal boredom, or such horror it's better not to think about it. At last I made up my mind and changed into a bumpkin, a tramp with a knapsack, and left for good: Rus', adieu! Here a kindred spirit, a Water-Sprite, gave me a hand. Poor fellow was on the run too. He kept marveling, kept saying: – what times are upon us, a real calamity! And even if, in olden times, he had had his fun, used to lure people down (a hospitable one, he was!), in recompense how he petted and pampered them on the gold river bottom, with what songs he bewitched them! These days, he says, only dead men come floating by, floating in batches, enormous numbers of them, and the river's moisture is like blood, thick, warm, sticky, and there's nothing for him to breathe . . . And so he took me with him.

'He went off to knock about some distant sea, and put me ashore on a foggy coast – go, brother, find yourself some friendly foliage. But I found nothing, and ended up here in this foreign, terrifying city of stone. Thus I turned into a human, complete with proper starched collars and bootees, and I've even learned human talk . . .'

He fell silent. His eyes glistened like wet leaves, his arms were crossed, and, by the wavering light of the

The Wood-Sprite

drowning candle, some pale strands combed to the left shimmered so strangely.

'I know you too are pining,' his voice shimmered again, 'but your pining, compared to mine, my tempestuous, turbulent pining, is but the even breathing of one who is asleep. And think about it: not one of our Tribe is there left in Rus'. Some of us swirled away like wisps of fog, others scattered over the world. Our native rivers are melancholy, there is no frisky hand to splash up the moon-gleams. Silent are the orphaned bluebells that remain, by chance, unmown, the pale-blue *gusli* that once served my rival, the ethereal Field-Sprite, for his songs. The shaggy, friendly, household spirit, in tears, has forsaken your besmirched, humiliated home, and the groves have withered, the pathetically luminous, magically somber groves . . .

'It was we, Rus', who were your inspiration, your unfathomable beauty, your agelong enchantment! And we are all gone, gone, driven into exile by a crazed surveyor.

'My friend, soon I shall die, say something to me, tell me that you love me, a homeless phantom, come sit closer, give me your hand . . .'

The candle sputtered and went out. Cold fingers touched my palm. The familiar melancholy laugh pealed and fell still.

When I turned on the light there was no one in the armchair . . . No one! . . . Nothing was left but a wondrously subtle scent in the room, of birch, of humid moss . . .

Music

The entrance hall overflowed with coats of both sexes; from the drawing room came a rapid succession of piano notes. Victor's reflection in the hall mirror straightened the knot of a reflected tie. Straining to reach up, the maid hung his overcoat, but it broke loose, taking down two others with it, and she had to begin all over again.

Already walking on tiptoe, Victor reached the drawing room, whereupon the music at once became louder and manlier. At the piano sat Wolf, a rare guest in that house. The rest – some thirty people in all – were listening in a variety of attitudes, some with chin propped on fist, others sending cigarette smoke up toward the ceiling, and the uncertain lighting lent a vaguely picturesque quality to their immobility. From afar, the lady of the house, with an eloquent smile, indicated to Victor an unoccupied seat, a pretzel-backed little armchair almost in the shadow of the grand piano. He responded with self-effacing gestures – it's all right, it's all right, I can stand; presently, however, he began moving in the suggested direction, cautiously sat down, and cautiously folded his arms. The performer's wife, her mouth half-open, her eyes blinking fast, was about to turn the page; now she has turned it. A black forest of ascending notes, a slope, a gap, then a separate group of little trapezists in flight. Wolf had long, fair eyelashes; his translucent ears were of a delicate crimson hue; he struck the keys with extraordinary velocity and vigor and, in the lacquered depths of the open keyboard lid, the doubles of his hands were engaged in a ghostly, intricate, even somewhat clownish mimicry.

To Victor any music he did not know – and all he knew was a dozen conventional tunes – could be likened to the patter of a conversation in a strange tongue: in vain you strive to define at least the limits of the words, but everything slips and merges, so that the laggard ear begins to feel boredom. Victor tried to concentrate on listening, but soon caught himself watching Wolf's hands and their spectral reflections. When the sounds grew into insistent thunder, the performer's neck would swell, his widespread fingers tensed, and he emitted a faint grunt. At one point his wife got ahead of him; he arrested the page with an instant slap of his open left palm, then with incredible speed himself flipped it over, and already both hands were fiercely kneading the compliant keyboard again. Victor made a detailed study of the man: sharp-tipped nose, jutting eyelids, scar left by a boil on his neck, hair resembling blond fluff, broad-shouldered cut of black jacket. For a moment Victor tried to attend to the music again, but scarcely had he focused on it when his attention dissolved. He slowly turned away, fishing out his cigarette case, and began to examine the other guests. Among the strange faces he discovered some familiar ones – nice, chubby Kocharovsky over there – should

Music

I nod to him? He did, but overshot his mark: it was another acquaintance, Shmakov, who acknowledged the nod: I heard he was leaving Berlin for Paris – must ask him about it. On a divan, flanked by two elderly ladies, corpulent, red-haired Anna Samoylovna half-reclined with closed eyes, while her husband, a throat specialist, sat with his elbow propped on the arm of his chair. What is that glittering object he twirls in the fingers of his free hand? Ah yes, a pince-nez on a Chekhovian ribbon. Further, one shoulder in shadow, a hunchbacked, bearded man known to be a lover of music listened intently, an index finger stretched up against his temple. Victor could never remember his name and patronymic. Boris? No, that wasn't it. Borisovich? Not that either. More faces. Wonder if the Haruzins are here. Yes, there they are. Not looking my way. And in the next instant, immediately behind them, Victor saw his former wife.

At once he lowered his gaze, automatically tapping his cigarette to dislodge the ash that had not yet had time to form. From somewhere low down his heart rose like a fist to deliver an uppercut, drew back, struck again, then went into a fast, disorderly throb, contradicting the music and drowning it. Not knowing which way to look, he glanced askance at the pianist, but did not hear a sound: Wolf seemed to be pounding a silent keyboard. Victor's chest got so constricted that he had to straighten up and draw a deep breath; then, hastening back from a great distance, gasping for air, the music returned to life, and his heart resumed beating with a more regular rhythm.

They had separated two years before, in another town, where the sea boomed at night, and where they had lived since their marriage. With his eyes still cast down, he tried to ward off the thunder and rush of the past with trivial thoughts: for instance, that she must have observed him a few moments ago as, with long, noiseless, bobbing strides, he had tiptoed the whole length of the room to reach this chair. It was as if someone had caught him undressed or engaged in some idiotic occupation; and, while recalling how in his innocence he had glided and plunged under her gaze (hostile? derisive? curious?), he interrupted himself to consider if his hostess or anyone else in the room might be aware of the situation, and how had she got here, and whether she had come alone or with her new husband, and what he, Victor, ought to do: stay as he was or look her way? No, looking was still impossible; first he had to get used to her presence in this large but confining room – for the music had fenced them in and had become for them a kind of prison, where they were both fated to remain captive until the pianist ceased constructing and keeping up his vaults of sound.

What had he had time to observe in that brief glance of recognition a moment ago? So little: her averted eyes, her pale cheek, a lock of black hair, and, as a vague secondary character, beads or something around her neck. So little! Yet that careless sketch, that half-finished image already *was* his wife, and its momentary blend of gleam and shade already formed the unique entity which bore her name.

Music

How long ago it all seemed! He had fallen madly in love with her one sultry evening, under a swooning sky, on the terrace of the tennis-club pavilion, and, a month later, on their wedding night, it rained so hard you could not hear the sea. What bliss it had been. Bliss – what a moist, lapping, and plashing word, so alive, so tame, smiling and crying all by itself. And the morning after: those glistening leaves in the garden, that almost noiseless sea, that languid, milky, silvery sea.

Something had to be done about his cigarette butt. He turned his head, and again his heart missed a beat. Someone had stirred, blocking his view of her almost totally, and was taking out a handkerchief as white as death; but presently the stranger's elbow would go and she would reappear, yes, in a moment she would reappear. No, I can't bear to look. There's an ashtray on the piano.

The barrier of sounds remained just as high and impenetrable. The spectral hands in their lacquered depths continued to go through the same contortions. 'We'll be happy forever' – what melody in that phrase, what shimmer! She was velvet-soft all over, one longed to gather her up the way one could gather up a foal and its folded legs. Embrace her and fold her. And then what? What could one do to possess her completely? I love your liver, your kidneys, your blood cells. To this she would reply, 'Don't be disgusting.' They lived neither in luxury nor in poverty, and went swimming in the sea almost all year round. The jellyfish, washed up onto the shingly beach, trembled in the wind. The Crimean cliffs glistened in the spray. Once they saw fishermen carrying away the body of a drowned man; his bare feet, protruding from under the blanket, looked surprised. In the evenings she used to make cocoa.

He looked again. She was now sitting with downcast eyes, legs crossed, chin propped upon knuckles: she was very musical, Wolf must be playing some famous, beautiful piece. I won't be able to sleep for several nights, thought Victor as he contemplated her white neck and the soft angle of her knee. She wore a flimsy black dress, un-familiar to him, and her necklace kept catching the light. No, I won't be able to sleep, and I shall have to stop coming here. It has all been in vain: two years of straining and struggling, my peace of mind almost regained – now I must start all over again, trying to forget everything, everything that had already been almost forgotten, plus this evening on top of it. It suddenly seemed to him that she was looking at him furtively and he turned away.

The music must be drawing to a close. When they come, those stormy, gasping chords, it usually signifies that the end is near. Another intriguing word, *end* . . . Rend, impend . . . Thunder rending the sky, dust clouds of impending doom. With the coming of spring she became strangely unresponsive. She spoke almost without moving her lips. He would ask 'What is the matter with you?' 'Nothing. Nothing in particular.' Sometimes she would stare at him out of narrowed eyes, with an enigmatic expression. 'What *is* the matter?' 'Nothing.' By nightfall she would be as good as dead. You could not do anything with her, for, despite her being a small, slender woman, she would grow heavy and unwieldy, and as if made of stone. 'Won't you finally tell me what is the matter with you?' So it went for almost a month. Then, one morning – yes, it was the morning of her birthday – she said quite simply, as if she were talking about some trifle, 'Let's separate for a while. We can't go on like this.' The neighbors' little daughter burst into the room to show her kitten (the sole survivor of a litter that had been drowned). 'Go away, go away, later.' The little girl left. There was a long silence. After a while, slowly, silently, he began twisting her wrists – he longed to break all of her, to dislocate all her joints with loud cracks. She started to cry. Then he sat down at the table and pretended to read the newspaper. She went out into the garden, but soon returned. 'I can't keep it back any longer. I have to tell you everything.' And with an odd astonishment, as if discussing another woman, and being astonished at her, and inviting him to share her astonishment, she told it, told it all. The man in question was a burly, modest, and reserved fellow; he used to come for a game of whist, and liked to talk about artesian wells. The first time had been in the park, then at his place.

The rest is all very vague. I paced the beach till nightfall. Yes, the music does seem to be ending. When I slapped his face on the quay, he said, 'You'll pay dearly for this,' picked up his cap from the ground, and walked away. I did not say goodbye to her. How silly it would have been to think of killing her. Live on, live. Live as you are living now; as you are sitting now, sit like that forever. Come, look at me, I implore you, please, please look. I'll forgive you everything, because someday we must all die, and then we shall know everything, and everything will be forgiven – so why put it off? Look at me, look at me, turn your eyes, *my* eyes, my darling eyes. No. Finished.

The last many-clawed, ponderous chords – another, and just enough breath left for one more, and, after this concluding chord, with which the music seemed to have surrendered its soul entirely, the performer took aim and, with feline precision, struck one simple, quite separate little golden note. The musical barrier dissolved. Applause. Wolf said, 'It's been a very long time since I last played this.' Wolf's wife said, 'It's been a long time, you know, since my husband last played this piece.' Advancing upon him, crowding him, nudging him with his paunch, the throat specialist said to Wolf: 'Marvelous! I have always maintained that's the best thing he ever wrote. I think that toward the end you modernize the color of sound just a bit too much. I don't know if I make myself clear, but, you see—'

Victor was looking in the direction of the door. There, a slightly built, black-haired lady with a helpless smile was taking leave of the hostess, who kept exclaiming in surprise, 'I won't hear of it, we're all going to have tea now, and then we're going to hear a singer.' But she kept on smiling helplessly and made her way to the door, and Victor realized that the music, which before had seemed a narrow dungeon where, shackled together by the resonant sounds, they had been compelled to sit face-to-face some twenty feet apart, had actually been incredible bliss, a magic glass dome that had embraced and imprisoned him and her, had made it possible for him to breathe the same air as she; and now everything had been broken and scattered, she was disappearing through the door, Wolf had shut the piano, and the enchanting captivity could not be restored.

She left. Nobody seemed to have noticed anything. He was greeted by a man named Boke who said in a gentle voice, 'I kept watching you. What a reaction to music! You know, you looked so bored I felt sorry for you. Is it possible that you are so completely indifferent to it?'

'Why, no. I wasn't bored,' Victor answered awkwardly. 'It's just that I have no ear for music, and that makes me a poor judge. By the way, what was it he played?'

'What you will,' said Boke in the apprehensive whisper of a rank outsider. '"Maiden's Prayer", or the "Kreutzer Sonata". Whatever you will.'

Perfection

'Now then, here we have two lines,' he would say to David in a cheery, almost rapturous voice as if to have two lines were a rare fortune, something one could be proud of. David was gentle but dullish. Watching David's ears evolve a red glow, Ivanov foresaw he would often appear in David's dreams, thirty or forty years hence: human dreams do not easily forget old grudges.

Fair-haired and thin, wearing a yellow sleeveless jersey held close by a leather belt, with scarred naked knees and a wristwatch whose crystal was protected by a prison-window grating, David sat at the table in a most uncomfortable position, and kept tapping his teeth with the blunt end of his fountain pen. He was doing badly at school, and it had become necessary to engage a private tutor.

'Let us now turn to the second line,' Ivanov continued with the same studied cheeriness. He had taken his degree in geography but his special knowledge could not be put to any use: dead riches, a highborn pauper's magnificent manor. How beautiful, for instance, are ancient charts! Viatic maps of the Romans, elongated, ornate, with snakelike marginal stripes representing canal-shaped seas; or those drawn in ancient

Alexandria, with England and Ireland looking like two little sausages; or again, maps of medieval Christendom, crimson-and-grass-colored, with the paradisian Orient at the top and Jerusalem – the world's golden navel – in the center. Accounts of marvelous pilgrimages: that traveling monk comparing the Jordan to a little river in his native Chernigov, that envoy of the Tsar reaching a country where people strolled under yellow parasols, that merchant from Tver picking his way through a dense '*zhengel*', his Russian for 'jungle,' full of monkeys, to a torrid land ruled by a naked prince. The islet of the known universe keeps growing: new hesitant contours emerge from the fabulous mists, slowly the globe disrobes – and lo, out of the remoteness beyond the seas, looms South America's shoulder and from their four corners blow fat-cheeked winds, one of them wearing spectacles.

But let us forget the maps. Ivanov had many other joys and eccentricities. He was lanky, swarthy, none too young, with a permanent shadow cast on his face by a black beard that had once been permitted to grow for a long time, and had then been shaven off (at a barbershop in Serbia, his first stage of expatriation): the slightest indulgence made that shadow revive and begin to bristle. Throughout a dozen years of émigré life, mostly in Berlin, he had remained faithful to starched collars and cuffs; his deteriorating shirts had an outdated tongue in front to be buttoned to the top of his long underpants. Of late he had been obliged to wear constantly his old formal black suit with braid piping along the lapels (all

Perfection

his other clothes having rotted away); and occasionally, on an overcast day, in a forbearing light, it seemed to him that he was dressed with sober good taste. Some sort of flannel entrails were trying to escape from his necktie, and he was forced to trim off parts of them, but could not bring himself to excise them altogether.

He would set out for his lesson with David at around three in the afternoon, with a somewhat unhinged, bouncing gait, his head held high. He would inhale avidly the young air of the early summer, rolling his large Adam's apple, which in the course of the morning had already fledged. On one occasion a youth in leather leggings attracted Ivanov's absent gaze from the opposite sidewalk by means of a soft whistle, and, throwing up his own chin, kept it up for a distance of a few steps: thou shouldst correct thy fellow man's oddities. Ivanov, however, misinterpreted that didactic mimicry and, assuming that something was being pointed out to him overhead, looked trustingly even higher than was his wont – and, indeed, three lovely cloudlets, holding each other by the hand, were drifting diagonally across the sky; the third one fell slowly behind, and its outline, and the outline of the friendly hand still stretched out to it, slowly lost their graceful significance.

During those first warm days everything seemed beautiful and touching: the leggy little girls playing hopscotch on the sidewalk, the old men on the benches, the green confetti that sumptuous lindens scattered every time the air stretched its invisible limbs. He felt lonesome and stifled in black. He would take off his hat and stand still for a moment looking around. Sometimes, as he looked at a chimney sweep (that indifferent carrier of other people's luck, whom women in passing touched with superstitious fingers), or at an airplane overtaking a cloud, Ivanov daydreamed about the many things that he would never get to know closer, about professions that he would never practice, about a parachute, opening like a colossal corolla, or the fleeting, speckled world of automobile racers, about various images of happiness, about the pleasures of very rich people amid very picturesque natural surroundings. His thought fluttered and walked up and down the glass pane which for as long as he lived would prevent him from having direct contact with the world. He had a passionate desire to experience everything, to attain and touch everything, to let the dappled voices, the bird calls, filter through his being and to enter for a moment into a passerby's soul as one enters the cool shade of a tree. His mind would be preoccupied with unsolvable problems: How and where do chimney sweeps wash after work? Has anything changed about that forest road in Russia that a moment ago he had recalled so vividly?

When, at last, late as usual, he went up in the elevator, he would have a sensation of slowly growing, stretching upward, and, after his head had reached the sixth floor, of pulling up his legs like a swimmer. Then, having reverted to normal length, he would enter David's bright room.

During lessons David liked to fiddle with things but otherwise remained fairly attentive. He had been raised abroad and spoke Russian with difficulty and boredom, and, when faced with the necessity of expressing something important, or when talking to his mother, the Russian wife of a Berlin businessman, would immediately switch to German. Ivanov, whose knowledge of the local language was poor, expounded mathematics in Russian, while the textbook was, of course, in German, and this produced a certain amount of confusion. As he watched the boy's ears, edged with fair down, he tried to imagine the degree of tedium and detestation he must arouse in David, and this distressed him. He saw himself from the outside – a blotchy complexion, a *feu du rasoir* rash, a shiny black jacket, stains on its sleeve cuffs – and caught his own falsely animated tone, the throat-clearing noises he made, and even that sound which could not reach David – the blundering but dutiful beat of his long-ailing heart. The lesson came to an end, the boy would hurry to show him something, such as an automobile catalogue, or a camera, or a cute little screw found in the street – and then Ivanov did his best to give proof of intelligent participation – but, alas, he never had been on intimate terms with the secret fraternity of man-made things that goes under the name technology, and this or that inexact observation of his would make David fix him with puzzled pale-gray eyes and quickly take back the object which seemed to be whimpering in Ivanov's hands.

And yet David was not untender. His indifference to the unusual could be explained – for I, too, reflected Ivanov, must have appeared to be a stolid and dryish lad, I who never shared with anyone my loves, my fancies and fears. All that my childhood expressed was an excited little monologue addressed to itself. One might construct the following syllogism: a child is the most perfect type of humanity; David is a child; David is perfect. With such adorable eyes as he has, a boy cannot possibly keep thinking only about the prices of various mechanical gadgets or about how to save enough trading stamps to obtain fifty pfennigs' worth of free merchandise at the store. He must be saving up something else too: bright childish impressions whose paint remains on the fingertips of the mind. He keeps silent about it just as I kept silent. But if several decades later – say, in 1970 (how they resemble telephone numbers, those distant years!), he will happen to see again that picture now hanging above his bed – Bonzo devouring a tennis ball – what a jolt he will feel, what light, what amazement at his own existence. Ivanov was not entirely wrong, David's eyes, indeed, were not devoid of a certain dreaminess; but it was the dreaminess of concealed mischief.

Enters David's mother. She has yellow hair and a highstrung temperament. The day before she was studying Spanish; today she subsists on orange juice. 'I would like to speak to you. Stay seated, please. Go away, David. The lesson is over? David, go. This is what I want to say. His vacation is coming soon. It would be appropriate to take him to the seaside. Regrettably, I shan't be able to go myself. Would you be willing to take him along? I trust you, and he listens to you. Above all, I want him to speak Russian more often. Actually, he's nothing but a little *Sportsmann* as are all modern kids. Well, how do you look at it?'

With doubt. But Ivanov did not voice his doubt. He had last seen the sea in 1912, eighteen years ago when he was a university student. The resort was Hungerburg in the province of Estland. Pines, sand, silvery-pale water far away – oh, how long it took one to reach it, and then how long it took it to reach up to one's knees! It would be the same Baltic Sea, but a different shore. However, the last time I went swimming was not at Hungerburg but in the river Luga. Muzhiks came running out of the water, frog-legged, hands crossed over their private parts: *pudor agrestis*. Their teeth chattered as they pulled on their shirts over their wet bodies. Nice to go bathing in the river toward evening, especially under a warm rain that makes silent circles, each spreading and encroaching upon the next, all over the water. But I like to feel underfoot the presence of the bottom. How hard to put on again one's socks and shoes without muddying the soles of one's feet! Water in one's ear: keep hopping on one foot until it spills out like a tickly tear.

The day of departure soon came. 'You will be frightfully hot in those clothes,' remarked David's mother by way of farewell as she glanced at Ivanov's black suit (worn in mourning for his other defunct things). The train was crowded, and his new, soft collar (a slight compromise, a summer treat) turned gradually into a tight clammy compress. Happy David, his hair neatly trimmed, with one small central tuft playing in the wind, his open-necked shirt aflutter, stood, at the corridor window, peering out, and on curves the semicircles of the front cars would become visible, with the heads of passengers who leaned on the lowered frames. Then the train, its bell ringing, its elbows working ever so rapidly, straightened out again to enter a beech forest.

The house was located at the rear of the little seaside town, a plain two-storied house with red-currant shrubs in the yard, which a fence separated from the dusty road. A tawny-bearded fisherman sat on a log, slitting his eyes in the low sun as he tarred his net. His wife led them upstairs. Terra-cotta floors, dwarf furniture. On the wall, a fair-sized fragment of an airplane propeller: 'My husband used to work at the airport.' Ivanov unpacked his scanty linen, his razor, and a dilapidated volume of Pushkin's works in the Panafidin edition. David freed from its net a varicolored ball that went jumping about and from sheer exuberance only just missed knocking a horned shell off its shelf. The landlady brought tea and some flounder. David was in a hurry. He could not wait to get a look at the sea. The sun had already begun to set.

When they came down to the beach after a fifteen-minute walk, Ivanov instantly became conscious of an acute discomfort in his chest, a sudden tightness followed by a sudden void, and out on the smooth, smoke-blue sea a small boat looked black and appallingly alone. Its imprint began to appear on whatever he looked at, then dissolved in the air. Because now the dust of twilight dimmed everything around, it seemed to him that his eyesight was dulled, while his legs felt strangely weakened by the squeaky touch of the sand.

Perfection

From somewhere came the playing of an orchestra, and its every sound, muted by distance, seemed to be corked up; breathing was difficult. David chose a spot on the beach and ordered a wicker cabana for next day. The way back was uphill; Ivanov's heart now drifted away, then hurried back to perform anyhow what was expected of it, only to escape again, and through all this pain and anxiety the nettles along the fences smelled of Hungerburg.

David's white pajamas. For reasons of economy Ivanov slept naked. At first the earthen cold of the clean sheets made him feel even worse, but then repose brought relief. The moon groped its way to the washstand, selected there one facet of a tumbler, and started to crawl up the wall. On that and on the following nights, Ivanov thought vaguely of several matters at once, imagining among other things that the boy who slept in the bed next to his was his own son. Ten years before, in Serbia, the only woman he had ever loved – another man's wife – had become pregnant by him. She suffered a miscarriage and died the next night, deliring and praying. He would have had a son, a little fellow about David's age. When in the morning David prepared to pull on his swimming trunks, Ivanov was touched by the way his café-au-lait tan (already acquired on a Berlin lakeside) abruptly gave way to a childish whiteness below the waist. He was about to forbid the boy to go from house to beach with nothing on but those trunks, and was a little taken aback, and did not immediately give in, when David began to argue, with the whining intonations of German astonishment, that he had done so at another resort and that everyone did it. As to Ivanov, he languished on the beach in the sorrowful image of a city dweller. The sun, the sparkling blue, made him seasick. A hot tingling ran over the top of his head under his fedora, he felt as if he were being roasted alive, but he would not even dispense with his jacket, not only because as is the case with many Russians, it would embarrass him to 'appear in his braces in the presence of ladies,' but also because his shirt was too badly frayed. On the third day he suddenly gathered up his courage and, glancing furtively around from under his brows, took off his shoes. He settled at the bottom of a crater dug by David, with a newspaper sheet spread under his elbow, and listened to the tight snapping of the gaudy flags, or else peered over the sandy brink with a kind of tender envy at a thousand brown corpses felled in various attitudes by the sun; one girl was especially magnificent, as if cast in metal, tanned to the point of blackness, with amazingly light eyes and with fingernails as pale as a monkey's. Looking at her he tried to imagine what it felt like to be so sun-baked.

On obtaining permission for a dip, David would noisily swim off while Ivanov walked to the edge of the surf to watch his charge and to jump back whenever a wave spreading farther than its predecessors threatened to douse his trousers. He recalled a fellow student in Russia, a close friend of his, who had the knack of pitching pebbles so as to have them glance off the water's surface two, three, four times, but when he tried to demonstrate it to David, the projectile pierced the surface with a loud plop, and David laughed, and made a nice flat stone perform not four but at least six skips.

A few days later, during a spell of absentmindedness (his eyes had strayed, and it was too late when he caught up with them), Ivanov read a postcard that David had begun writing to his mother and had left lying on the window ledge. David wrote that his tutor was probably ill for he never went swimming. That very day Ivanov took extraordinary measures: he acquired a black bathing suit and, on reaching the beach, hid in the cabana, undressed gingerly, and pulled on the cheap shop-smelling stockinet garment. He had a moment of melancholy embarrassment when, pale-skinned and hairy-legged, he emerged into the sunlight. David, however, looked at him with approval. 'Well!' exclaimed Ivanov with devil-may-care jauntiness, 'here we go!' He went in up to his knees, splashed some water on his head, then walked on with outspread arms, and the higher the water rose, the deadlier became the spasm that contracted his heart. At last, closing his ears with his thumbs, and covering his eyes with the rest of his fingers, he immersed himself in a crouching position. The stabbing chill compelled him to get promptly out of the water. He lay down on the sand, shivering and filled to the brim of his being with ghastly, unresolvable anguish. After a while the sun warmed him, he revived, but from then on forswore sea bathing. He felt too lazy to dress; when he closed his eyes tightly, optical spots glided against a red background, Martian canals kept intersecting, and, the moment he parted his lids, the wet silver of the sun started to palpitate between his lashes.

The inevitable took place. By evening, all those parts of his body that had been exposed turned into a symmetrical archipelago of fiery pain. 'Today, instead of going to the beach, we shall take a walk in the woods,' he said to the boy on the morrow. *'Ach, nein,'* wailed David. 'Too much sun is bad for the health,' said Ivanov. 'Oh, please!' insisted David in great dismay. But Ivanov stood his ground.

The forest was dense. Geometrid moths, matching the bark in coloration, flew off the tree trunks. Silent David walked reluctantly. 'We should cherish the woods,' Ivanov said in an attempt to divert his pupil. 'It was the first habitat of man. One fine day man left the jungle of primitive intimations for the sunlit glade of reason. Those bilberries appear to be ripe, you have my permission to taste them. Why do you sulk? Try to understand: one should vary one's pleasures. And one should not overindulge in sea bathing. How often it happens that a careless bather dies of sun stroke or heart failure!'

Ivanov rubbed his unbearably burning and itching back against a tree trunk and continued pensively: 'While admiring nature at a given locality, I cannot help thinking of countries that I shall never see. Try to imagine, David, that this is not Pomerania but a Malayan forest. Look about you: you'll presently see the rarest of birds fly past, Prince Albert's paradise bird, whose head is adorned with a pair of long plumes consisting of blue oriflammes.' *'Ach, quatsch,'* responded David dejectedly.

Perfection

'In Russian you ought to say *"erundá"*. Of course, it's nonsense, we are not in the mountains of New Guinea. But the point is that with a bit of imagination – if, God forbid, you were someday to go blind or be imprisoned, or were merely forced to perform, in appalling poverty, some hopeless, distasteful task, you might remember this walk we are taking today in an ordinary forest as if it had been – how shall I say? – fairy-tale ecstasy.'

At sundown dark-pink clouds fluffed out above the sea. With the dulling of the sky they seemed to rust, and a fisherman said it would rain tomorrow, but the morning turned out to be marvelous and David kept urging his tutor to hurry, but Ivanov was not feeling well; he longed to stay in bed and think of remote and vague semievents illumined by memory on only one side, of some pleasant smoke-gray things that might have happened once upon a time, or drifted past quite close to him in life's field of vision, or else had appeared to him in a recent dream. But it was impossible to concentrate on them, they all somehow slipped away to one side, half-turning to him with a kind of friendly and mysterious slyness but gliding away relentlessly, as do those transparent little knots that swim diagonally in the vitreous humor of the eye. Alas, he had to get up, to pull on his socks, so full of holes that they resembled lace mittens. Before leaving the house he put on David's dark-yellow sunglasses – and the sun swooned amid a sky dying a turquoise death, and the morning light upon the porch steps acquired a sunset tinge. David, his naked back amber-colored, ran ahead, and when Ivanov called to him, he shrugged his shoulders in irritation. 'Do not run away,' Ivanov said wearily. His horizon was narrowed by the glasses, he was afraid of a sudden automobile.

The street sloped sleepily toward the sea. Little by little his eyes became used to the glasses, and he ceased to wonder at the sunny day's khaki uniform. At the turn of the street he suddenly half-remembered something – something extraordinarily comforting and strange – but it immediately dissolved, and the turbulent sea air constricted his chest. The dusky flags flapped excitedly, pointing all in the same direction, though nothing was happening there yet. Here is the sand, here is the dull splash of the sea. His ears felt plugged up, and when he inhaled through the nose a rumble started in his head, and something bumped into a membranous dead end. I've lived neither very long nor very well, reflected Ivanov. Still it would be a shame to complain; this alien world is beautiful, and I would feel happy right now if only I could recall that wonderful, wonderful – what? What was it?

He lowered himself onto the sand. David began busily repairing with a spade the sand wall where it had crumbled slightly. 'Is it hot or cool today?' asked Ivanov. 'Somehow I cannot decide.' Presently David threw down the spade and said, 'I'll go for a swim.' 'Sit still for a moment,' said Ivanov. 'I must gather my thoughts. The sea will not run away.' '*Please* let me go!' pleaded David.

Ivanov raised himself on one elbow and surveyed the waves. They were large and humpbacked; nobody was bathing at that spot; only much farther to the left a dozen orange-capped heads bobbed and were carried off to one side in unison. 'Those waves,' said Ivanov with a sigh, and then added: 'You may paddle a little, but don't go beyond a *sazhen*. A *sazhen* equals about two meters.'

He sank his head, propping one cheek, grieving, computing indefinite measures of life, of pity, of happiness. His shoes were already full of sand, he took them off with slow hands, then was again lost in thought, and again those evasive little knots began to swim across his field of vision – and how he longed, how he longed to recall – A sudden scream. Ivanov stood up.

Amid yellow-blue waves, far from the shore, flitted David's face, and his open mouth was like a dark hole. He emitted a spluttering yell, and vanished. A hand appeared for a moment and vanished too. Ivanov threw off his jacket. 'I'm coming,' he shouted. 'I'm coming. Hold on!' He splashed through the water, lost his footing, his ice-cold trousers stuck to his shins. It seemed to him that David's head came up again for an instant. Then a wave surged, knocking off Ivanov's hat, blinding him; he wanted to take off his glasses, but his agitation, the cold, the numbing weakness, prevented him from doing so. He realized that in its retreat the wave had dragged him a long way from the shore. He started to swim trying to catch sight of David. He felt enclosed in a tight painfully cold sack, his heart was straining unbearably. All at once a rapid something passed through him, a flash of fingers rippling over piano keys – and *this* was the very thing he had been trying to recall throughout the morning. He came out on a stretch of sand. Sand, sea, and air were of an odd, faded, opaque tint, and everything was perfectly still. Vaguely he reflected that twilight must have come, and that David had perished a long time ago, and he felt what he knew from earthly life – the poignant heat of tears. Trembling and bending toward the ashen sand, he wrapped himself tighter in the black cloak with the snake-shaped brass fastening that he had seen on a student friend, a long, long time ago, on an autumn day – and he felt so sorry for David's mother, and wondered what would he tell her. It is not my fault, I did all I could to save him, but I am a poor swimmer, and I have a bad heart, and he drowned. But there was something amiss about these thoughts, and when he looked around once more and saw himself in the desolate mist all alone with no David beside him, he understood that if David was not with him, David was not dead.

Only then were the clouded glasses removed. The dull mist immediately broke, blossomed with marvelous colors, all kinds of sounds burst forth – the rote of the sea, the clapping of the wind, human cries – and there was David standing, up to his ankles in bright water, not knowing what to do, shaking with fear, not daring to explain that he had not been drowning, that he had struggled in jest – and farther out people were diving, groping through the water, then looking at each other with bulging eyes, and diving anew, and returning empty-handed, while others shouted to them from the shore, advising them to search a little to the left; and a fellow with a Red Cross armband was running along

Perfection

the beach, and three men in sweaters were pushing into the water a boat grinding against the shingle; and a bewildered David was being led away by a fat woman in a pince-nez, the wife of a veterinarian, who had been expected to arrive on Friday but had had to postpone his vacation, and the Baltic Sea sparkled from end to end, and, in the thinned-out forest, across a green country road, there lay, still breathing, freshly cut aspens; and a youth, smeared with soot, gradually turned white as he washed under the kitchen tap, and black parakeets flew above the eternal snows of the New Zealand mountains; and a fisherman, squinting in the sun, was solemnly predicting that not until the ninth day would the waves surrender the corpse.

PENGUIN ARCHIVE

H. G. Wells *The Time Machine*
M. R. James *The Stalls of Barchester Cathedral*
Jane Austen *The History of England by a Partial, Prejudiced and Ignorant Historian*
Edgar Allan Poe *Hop-Frog*
Virginia Woolf *The New Dress*
Antoine de Saint-Exupéry *Night Flight*
Oscar Wilde *A Poet Can Survive Everything But a Misprint*
George Orwell *Can Socialists be Happy?*
Dorothy Parker *Horsie*
D. H. Lawrence *Odour of Chrysanthemums*
Homer *The Wrath of Achilles*
Emily Brontë *No Coward Soul Is Mine*
Romain Gary *Lady L.*
Charles Dickens *The Chimes*
Dante *Hell*
Georges Simenon *Stan the Killer*
F. Scott Fitzgerald *The Rich Boy*
Katherine Mansfield *A Dill Pickle*
Fyodor Dostoyevsky *The Dream of a Ridiculous Man*

Franz Kafka *A Hunger-Artist*
Leo Tolstoy *Family Happiness*
Karen Blixen *The Dreaming Child*
Federico García Lorca *Cicada!*
Vladimir Nabokov *Revenge*
Albert Camus *A Short Guide to Towns Without a Past*
Muriel Spark *The Driver's Seat*
Carson McCullers *Reflections in a Golden Eye*
Wu Cheng'en *Monkey King Makes Havoc in Heaven*
Friedrich Nietzsche *Ecce Homo*
Laurie Lee *A Moment of War*
Roald Dahl *Lamb to the Slaughter*
Frank O'Connor *The Genius*
James Baldwin *The Fire Next Time*
Hermann Hesse *Strange News from Another Planet*
Gertrude Stein *Paris France*
Seneca *Why I am a Stoic*
Snorri Sturluson *The Prose Edda*
Elizabeth Gaskell *Lois the Witch*
Sei Shōnagon *A Lady in Kyoto*
Yasunari Kawabata *Thousand Cranes*
Jack Kerouac *Tristessa*
Arthur Schnitzler *A Confirmed Bachelor*
Chester Himes *All God's Chillun Got Pride*

Gérard de Nerval *October Nights*
Rumi *Where Everything is Music*
H. P. Lovecraft *The Shadow Out of Time*
Christina Rossetti *To Read and Dream*
Dambudzo Marechera *The House of Hunger*
Andy Warhol *Beauty*
Maurice Leblanc *The Escape of Arsène Lupin*
Eileen Chang *Jasmine Tea*
Irmgard Keun *After Midnight*
Walter Benjamin *Unpacking My Library*
Epictetus *Whatever is Rational is Tolerable*
Ota Pavel *How I Came to Know Fish*
César Aira *An Episode in the Life of a Landscape Painter*
Hafez *I am a Bird from Paradise*
Clarice Lispector *The Burned Sinner and the Harmonious Angels*
Maryse Condé *Tales from the Heart*
Audre Lorde *Coal*
Mary Gaitskill *Secretary*
Tove Ditlevsen *The Umbrella*
June Jordan *Passion*
Antonio Tabucchi *Requiem*
Alexander Lernet-Holenia *Baron Bagge*
Wang Xiaobo *The Maverick Pig*

Bram Stoker *The Burial of the Rats*
Czesław Miłosz *Rescue*
Hans Christian Andersen *The Emperor's New Clothes*
Bohumil Hrabal *Closely Watched Trains*
Italo Calvino *Under the Jaguar Sun*
Stanislaw Lem *The Seventh Voyage*
Shirley Jackson *The Daemon Lover*
Stefan Zweig *Chess*
Kate Chopin *The Story of an Hour*
Allen Ginsberg *Sunflower Sutra*
Rabindranath Tagore *The Broken Nest*
Søren Kierkegaard *The Seducer's Diary*
Mary Shelley *Transformation*
Nikolai Leskov *Night Owls*
Willa Cather *A Lost Lady*
Emilia Pardo Bazán *The Lady Bandit*
W. B. Yeats *Sailing to Byzantium*
Margaret Cavendish *The Blazing World*
Lafcadio Hearn *Some Japanese Ghosts*
Sarah Orne Jewett *The Country of the Pointed Firs*
Vincent van Gogh *For Art and for Life*
Dylan Thomas *Do Not Go Gentle Into That Good Night*
Mikhail Bulgakov *A Dog's Heart*
Saadat Hasan Manto *The Price of Freedom*